CW00666330

MAGIC'S TORMENT

SATAN'S LEGACY MC

ANDI RHODES

BLUE JOURNEY PUBLISHING

Also by Andi Rhodes

Piston

Greaser

Riker

Trainwreck

Squirrel

Gibson

Satan's Legacy MC

Snow's Angel

Toga's Demons

Magic's Torment

SATAN'S LEGACY MC

DENVER, CO CHAPTER

What the patch binds together,
let no force tear apart.
Satan's Legacy now and forever.

PROLOGUE
MAGIC

Three years ago...

"You don't have to do this."

I yank the rope tighter around my prey's wrists, binding him to the chair, and ignore him. I already have Laney's pleading cries stuck in my head. She begged me not to follow my president's orders to kill this man. Even if I didn't always do exactly as I'm instructed, I wouldn't have listened to Laney. She's my president's sister, not my boss. Besides, she was acting out of pure emotion.

"You know I do," I snap, punctuating my words with a yank on the rope around his ankles.

I'd prefer to use handcuffs, but I can't guarantee those would be destroyed by fire. When I walk out of this house, nothing can trace back to me or Satan's Legacy MC. It must look like an accident.

"I'll toss the papers," he pleads as I stand up. "I swear I will."

Normally, I love hearing my victims beg. Is there any

sweeter sound than that of the cries of someone who knows they're going to die even as they cling to a thin thread of hope? Not much.

"The papers have already been destroyed," I tell him and shake my head. "Did you really think you were going to get away with trying to take your son away from his mother?"

"She's not his mother!" he shouts, spit mixed with blood flying from his mouth.

I throw my head back and laugh, although there's little humor in it. This man is delusional. When I sober, I lean over him.

"She's the only parent he's ever known," I snarl. "Shiloh might not look like Laney, and he may not have her blood running through his veins, but she *is* his mother. She's the one who reads to him at bedtime, who changed his diapers, who worries when he's sick and cuddles him when he cries."

"Oh my God, I get it now," he taunts. "You think if you save Laney from me, you'll finally be able to have her all to yourself."

"Shut up," I bark just before my fist connects with his nose.

The sound of bone shattering centers me, fuels the rage I'm trying so hard to keep in check. I'm standing in a house in the middle of a residential street, surrounded by potential witnesses. And the longer I'm here, the harder it's getting to keep my voice low enough, so neighbors won't hear.

"If you kill me, you'll never get her," he sneers, his teeth stained crimson.

I take a step away from him and a few deep breaths. So

what if he figured out I have a crush on Laney? He's going to be dead, so that's info he'll take to his grave.

If he figured it out, others can too.

There's nothing to figure out. Laney is sexy as fuck, badass to her core while being sweet as cotton candy... and she's also my president's little sister. Which means she's off limits.

I shake the image of Laney out of my head and refocus on the man in front of me. He's my target, my intended victim. Laney can't factor in right now.

But she does. Especially now.

I bend over and pull the knife out of my boot before holding it to his throat. It takes every ounce of self-control I possess not to say fuck it and slice through his jugular. Or better yet, plunge it into his stomach and open him up like a gutted fish.

"She might not see it now, but killing you is the best thing that can happen to her and Shiloh."

"Keep telling yourself that."

My muscles burn to do what they're used to. Kill. Maim. Torture. I fight the urge, but barely. Afraid I'll use the knife, I slide it back into my boot, and then reach into my pocket for my Zippo.

I hold the lighter to his chin after flicking it to life. He tries to back away, but he can't. Fear registers on his face for what seems like the hundredth time since he walked into his kitchen to find me standing there.

"You're going to burn for your sins," I growl as I tip the flame to touch his blood-stained shirt.

It takes less than a second for his clothes to catch and his screams to pierce the air. I land one last punch that knocks him out, and then I take off.

When I get outside, I make sure to walk at a normal

pace so I don't draw attention to myself. By the time I reach my Harley, which I parked two blocks away, sirens and the exquisite smell of smoke fill the air.

Laney

"WE'RE *in need of an emergency placement for a four-month-old little boy. He was dropped off at the—"*

"Yes."

"Excuse me?"

"Yes, I'll take him."

"Don't you want more details?"

"Do they matter? I mean, I signed up to be a foster parent for a reason. This baby needs a home, and I can provide him that."

"True, but there are some things you should know."

Unease settles in my gut, but I push it aside. I meant what I said. I can give this little boy a good home with lots of love. But maybe the social worker is right. Maybe I can provide a better home if I know exactly what the circumstances are.

"Okay, what do I need to know?"

"For starters, he was abandoned at the fire station this evening. There was a note attached to his blanket that said he was being left by his mother because she couldn't take care of him. His birth certificate was also with him, so we know his name is Shiloh. We did a background check on the mother, and it turns out she's got quite the criminal history... mostly drug related. It's our assumption that her addiction took precedence over her son."

"And the father?" I ask. "What about him?"

"No father listed. We'll take all the necessary steps to locate him, but I'm not hopeful. We've spoken to the mother's family,

and none of them are willing or able to take him in, which is why I'm calling you. We need a placement for Shiloh. It could be temporary and that's always how we go into these things. Our goal is to reunite the family."

"But it could be long term?" I ask, hope tinging my tone.

"It could be, yes."

I shake my head to dislodge the memory and stare at my son. Shiloh is sound asleep in his bed, his blanket tucked under his chin. His little arm is wrapped tightly around his stuffed T-Rex, as it is every night when he goes to bed.

Shiloh rolls over in his sleep and settles in with his back toward me. It was a fight to get him into bed tonight because he kept asking for his dad. I tried to dodge the questions, but it wasn't easy. How do you tell your son that his dad is dead, or at least, will be dead, once the MC is done with him? Because he will be once Magic carries out Snow's orders.

A knock on my front door pulls my attention, and before leaving the bedroom, I lean over and kiss Shiloh on his five-year-old head. I gently close the door behind me, pausing for a moment to make sure he doesn't wake up at the sound of it clicking into place.

The knock reaches my ears again, and I mumble 'I'm coming' under my breath as I stride toward the front of the house. When I yank the door open, Magic is standing there, a scowl on his face.

"What's wrong?" I ask, fear wrapping its meaty fingers around my heart and squeezing.

Magic shakes his head. "Nothing."

I step aside, silently inviting Magic in. He passes me, his shoulder brushing mine, and plops down on the couch. His

5

giant frame seems to take up all the available space, and I wonder where I'm supposed to sit.

"I don't bite," Magic says.

"No shit." I tilt my head. "But you do kill."

"Only those who deserve it."

I cross the room and sit on the arm of the couch. "Like Cedric?"

"If ever anyone deserved to die by my hands, it's Cedric Milner."

I glance over my shoulder toward Shiloh's bedroom, almost as if to reassure myself that he's not standing there listening.

"So he's dead?"

Magic shifts to the opposite end of the couch and turns sideways to face me. "Laney, he's dead. He can't hurt you or Shiloh anymore."

I huff out a breath at his cavalier attitude. Cedric may have turned out to be a horrible person these last few months, but he wasn't always. Hell, I was engaged to the man.

"I can take the pain, Magic. What I can't take is Shiloh being ripped away from me," I say, trying to separate the man I loved from the man I came to fear.

Magic's lips lift. "And he can't do that either. I promise."

Air rushes past my lips. I nod. "At least something good will come of all this."

Silence fills the room, enveloping me in a feeling of safety, a feeling I haven't felt in months.

"So…" Magic begins, clearly not as comfortable with the quiet as I am. "Uh, where's Snow?"

Fresh anger rolls though me. "I made him leave a while ago."

"You're mad at him."

I stand and begin to pace. "Of course I'm mad at him. He's the one who brought Cedric into our lives."

"You know he wouldn't have done that if he had any clue how things would play out."

"That's bullshit and you know it. My brother was only thinking of himself... with his dick, I might add."

Magic chuckles, and the sound scratches at my brain like fingernails on a chalkboard. He must sense my disgust because he sobers.

"Laney, you can't blame him. Sure, he can be a horny bastard, but he would never intentionally do anything to hurt you." He shrugs. "Besides, it's not like he didn't suffer either."

I let out a humorless laugh. "Oh, right, I forgot. He had to dump his girlfriend. Poor Snow, won't be getting nightly blowjobs anymore."

"It's more than that," Magic counters. "He loved Marlene. I'm pretty sure he was going to ask her to be his ol' lady. But she betrayed him, just like Cedric betrayed you."

My control snaps, and I stomp toward Magic, rage wrapping around me like a suffocating blanket.

"Betrayal? Is that really what you think this is about?" I throw up my hands. "Betrayal is only the half of it, Magic. Cedric beat me." I lift my shirt, not even thinking about the fact that I'm exposing myself to a man who shouldn't be seeing any part of me other than what clothes don't cover. I point to a bruise on my stomach. "He did this with his fist." I point to one on my side. "And this was with his boot." I shove my shirt back into place. "Those are just two out of hundreds he gave me over the last few months. And then there's the mental bruises. The ones you can't see, the ones that won't heal so easily."

Magic's face is stone, his gaze still focused around my

stomach. I can't even begin to guess what he's thinking, but whatever it is, it makes him look scarier than I thought possible. Magic is the enforcer of Satan's Legacy MC, but he's also a big teddy bear when it comes to me and Shiloh. He can end a person's life without thinking twice about it, but he would also give *his* in the same manner.

"I didn't realize how bad it was," he finally says.

"Of course you didn't. I didn't want anyone to know. But today..." I rub my temples, trying to suppress the headache now blooming.

"Damn," Magic mumbles. "Makes me glad I didn't kill him before setting the fire."

"What?" I demand, fear hammering in my chest.

Magic closes the distance between us and rests his hands on my shoulders. "He's dead, Laney. I promise you that. I tied him down before I set the fire and left. He wasn't getting away."

Tears spring to my eyes, and I angrily wipe them away. I would love to say that I'm crying happy tears, but I can't. It's as if everything from the moment Cedric walked into our lives comes crashing down on me, and I simply cannot hold it up anymore.

"Aw, Laney, don't cry."

I turn my head away from Magic, hating that he's seeing this side of me. I'm normally a lot tougher than this. I've had to be with a big brother like Snow and the MC.

"C'mon, please," he pleads, discomfort in his voice. "I know you don't want to see Snow right now, but I'm gonna have to call him if you don't stop."

I shake my head violently, unable to slow the tears.

Magic shoves his hands in his pockets and rocks back on his heels. "Then tell me what to do. I don't know how to handle a crying woman."

A wet laugh escapes me, and I lift my head to look at Magic. He's just like my brother... clueless when it comes to women.

I swipe at my tears again while taking a few deep breaths to calm myself.

"Thank fucking Christ," Magic says. "I really didn't want to have to call Snow."

"If you had, you might have been sentenced to the same fate as Cedric."

"Damn, you really are mad at your brother."

"No shit, Sherlock. He put my son and me in danger. That's not easily forgivable."

"Understandable," he admits. "But try. If not for him or yourself, then for Shiloh. You're a family, and Shiloh loves his uncle. He's already lost one family. Don't make him lose another."

"That's harsh."

"It's reality," Magic counters. "I can't tell you how many families I've destroyed doing work for the club. And if I've learned anything from it, it's that every day matters because you never know when it's going to be your last."

I let Magic's words sink in. And while every inch of me knows he's right, there's a tiny piece of my stubborn streak that wants to hold onto the anger. Besides, anger is better than fear, better than feeling betrayed. I can handle anger.

Shiloh doesn't deserve an angry and bitter mom.

Shiloh. My son, my reason for breathing. He didn't ask for this. Hell, he doesn't even know what 'this' is. He has no clue that his life has irrevocably been changed, yet again. But he will... soon enough.

"Why don't you try to get some sleep?"

I lift my eyes to Magic's. "I..." I nod. "Yeah, that's probably a good idea."

9

"Do you want me to stick around? Or I can call Snow if you'd prefer he be here."

"Why would I want either of those things?"

"Because I can see the fear still swimming in your eyes. You're waiting for the other shoe to drop, and no matter what I say, I'm not going to be able to convince you that you're safe." When I open my mouth to protest, Magic holds a hand up. "Don't try to deny it. Hell, I don't blame you. I assure you that Cedric is dead, but I also know that hearing it and believing it way deep down are two very different things."

I shake my head. "No but thank you. I appreciate the offer, but Shiloh and I will be fine."

"Are you sure?"

Not at all.

"Absolutely. Go home and sleep in your own bed, Magic. Or go to the clubhouse and drink yourself stupid. Either way, just go. We're fine."

Magic looks at me like I'm trying to convince myself more than him. And he's not wrong about that. I don't think I'll get a wink of sleep tonight, but I'll be damned if I admit that.

"Okay." He shrugs. "If you're sure?"

I wrap my fingers around his bicep, enjoying the way his muscles bunch under my touch.

"Go."

I urge him toward the front door. He doesn't put up too much resistance, so I open the door and wait for him to step outside. When he turns around and looks at me, I rest my hand on my hip as if he's inconveniencing me.

"You'll call if you need anything?"

"Sure, Magic. I'll call."

"Okay." He turns away from me but looks over his shoulder. "Night, Laney."

"G'night."

I close the door and flip the lock before leaning against the wooden barrier. Magic's steps echo across the porch, but I don't hear him go down the steps. Shifting to the window, I pull aside the curtain.

And there's Magic, sitting in one of the two rocking chairs, staring out into the darkness. I want to march outside and demand he leave, but I can't ignore the amount of relief I feel that he's staying.

Feeling as safe as I can, I make my way through the house, turning off lights as I go. I debate on whether or not to unlock the front door, just in case Magic needs in. In the end, I keep it locked. Magic or no Magic, that's the smart thing to do.

After checking on Shiloh and reassuring myself he's still asleep, I go to my bedroom and crawl into bed. The covers provide a cocoon of safety, of comfort. I close my eyes, fully expecting to lie here for hours without falling asleep, but that's not what happens.

I think back over my conversation with Magic and his assurance that Cedric is dead. I think about Magic sitting in the rocking chair on my porch.

For tonight, at least, I'm safe, and within minutes, I'm also asleep.

CHAPTER 1

MAGIC

PRESENT DAY...

As I stretch my arms above my head, I stare out the bedroom window and silently groan at the darkness just beyond the glass. This is my routine and has been for the last year and a half. I stay over at Laney's and get up super early so I can slip out before Shiloh wakes up.

"Not yet," Laney mumbles from beside me.

She rolls over and throws her leg across both of mine. Her arm is next, and it rests on my bare chest. Both of us are naked, so I have to fight for control to not take her right here, right now.

I run a hand through her hair and sigh. "Sorry, Sweet Cheeks. I didn't make the rule, but I'll be damned if I'm not going to follow it."

Laney slowly sits up and scoots toward the headboard. "You know why Shiloh can't see you here. He can't keep a secret to save his life. I would love to broadcast our relationship to the world, but it would hurt you. The MC would vote you out, and then what?"

I shift so I'm sitting next to her. "I know you're right.

Doesn't mean I like it. I hate that we have to sneak around and that you're lying to your brother. Not to mention how hard it is to keep all the brothers from seeing what we don't want them to see. And the ol' ladies? They're the worst. I swear they know. Especially Fallon. She hasn't said anything, but she looks at me funny every time I'm around her. I don't know how much longer we'll be able to keep our fucking secret."

Laney brings her hand to rest on my shoulder. "We'll cross that bridge when we get there. I know they all need to find out sooner or later. But I'd like to enjoy you as long as I can."

Enjoy me? Now that's a damn good idea.

I turn away from Laney to glance at my phone to check the time. When I see that it's a little earlier than I thought, I throw the covers off of both of us and get out of bed. I reach for her ankles and savor the way she squeals when I yank her toward me.

"What are you doing?" she asks, but she doesn't fight me in the least.

I situate my hands in her armpits and lift her up. She immediately wraps her legs around my waist, and I almost blow my load from her body alone.

"We've got a little time, and I need a shower. Figured some company wouldn't hurt."

I wink at her, and her face turns pink. That's one of the things I love about Laney. Even though we've been together a while, she still gets embarrassed when I tease her. It's cute and such a one-eighty from how she is around everyone else. Laney is a ball-buster. It's almost as if she's afraid to let her vulnerable side out for anyone but me.

Laney slings her arms around my neck and uses that leverage to grind on my erection. While she's making it nearly impossible to remember my own name, I carry her to the adjoining bathroom.

I step into the tiled shower and turn the water on. Laney shrieks when the water hits her back, but as it warms up, she settles into me.

"Don't get too comfortable," I tell her before touching my tongue to her neck and licking a path to her ear.

"I won't, not until you're inside of me," she moans. "I'm always comfortable when you fill my pussy... in a euphoric sorta way."

"I'll give you euphoria," I growl in her ear as I back her against the gray-tiled wall.

Laney moans as our mouths fuse. Our tongues entangle in a primal rhythm, each of us devouring the other as if our lives depend on it. When Laney breaks the kiss, she stares me in the eyes.

"I'm gonna need you to fuck me. Now."

Her eyes darken, and her nostrils flare. Who am I to deny this woman anything she wants? I thrust inside her. Laney's walls spasm around me, hugging my cock in a grip that I don't think I'll ever tire of.

She throws her head back, banging it on the tile. Still, she doesn't miss a beat. Laney undulates, her hips matching mine with every deep thrust.

"Is this what you wanted?" I growl in her ear.

Laney nods frantically. I shift my hands from her ass to her thighs, lifting her legs slightly to get an angle I know will send her over the edge.

"Fuuuck," she groans.

She reaches between our bodies and stimulates her clit. Her moans become louder, more chaotic. Watching her like this, the way ecstasy plays across her face, is heaven. Everything with Laney is heaven... almost everything.

I slap a hand over her mouth, silently reminding her that she needs to be quiet. It won't do anyone any good if Shiloh hears us. Then our secret would be out for sure.

Laney bites down on my palm, but I don't move it. Instead, I let the sting fuel the fire already raging. Part of me wants to pull out and make her see the error of her ways, but I can't. Not when we're probably on borrowed time already. Besides, I don't think I can deprive myself of what's coming.

I pick up my pace, burying myself balls deep with each thrust. I need to come and so does Laney. Then I need to get the fuck out of here before it's too late.

"Come for me, Sweet Cheeks."

I remove my hand from her mouth and swat her hand out of the way so I can tease her clit. Holding her up with one hand, I fuck her as fast and as hard as I can while teasing her bundle of nerves to the breaking point.

Laney's pussy grips my dick harder as she moans out her pleasure. I don't bother silencing her now because I'm too engrossed in joining her.

"That's it," I say from behind clenched teeth.

Tingles race up my spine, and my balls tighten. My body shudders as I empty myself inside of Laney. When the feeling subsides, Laney continues to undulate her hips, clearly not finished. I increase pressure on her clit until her spasms wane, her body goes limp, and her head falls to my chest.

I stand there, still holding her up, not wanting to break the connection.

"Fuck, that was good," Laney mumbles against my chest.

"It always is."

Once we're out of the shower, Laney wraps a silk robe

around her body. Her usual post-satisfaction happiness is fading, and she finally lets her smile fall.

She turns to face me. "I hate this."

I step toward her and cup her cheek, rubbing my thumb over her skin. "I know. I do too."

"Is there ever going to come a time where we can tell people about us?"

I rest my forehead against hers. "Hey, where is this coming from?"

Laney shrugs. "I don't know. I'm just…" She sighs. "I'm tired of lying all the time."

"Look, if you want me to tell the brothers, I will. I'll do anything to make you happy. You know that."

"You do that, and you get voted out of Satan's Legacy." She shakes her head vehemently. "No, I can't let you do that."

Laney lifts her head and locks eyes with me. Resting her hands on my pecs, she says, "I'm sorry. I know this is how it has to be." She rises to her tip-toes and places a quick kiss to my lips. "I love you, Magic, and I don't like hiding that fact. But we have to. Someday, maybe that won't be the case."

It's on the tip of my tongue to tell her that's always going to be how it is if she insists I don't come clean to the others, but I resist spitting the words out. This situation isn't her fault. Nor mine. We're just two people who fell in love, despite the consequences.

"I for one, will take you anyway I can get you," I tell her. "I love you."

"I know you do." Laney takes a deep breath, and her cheeks puff out as she releases it. "But we're out of time for now."

She turns and opens the door. I walk into the bedroom

with her and search for my clothes. Finding them on the chair in the corner, I dress, all the while Laney watches me from where she sits on the edge of the bed. Her eyes register the same disappointment I felt when she covered herself up.

"Are you coming over tonight?" she asks as I slip my arms through my cut.

"Not sure yet. I think we've got something on the agenda, but if I'm back early, I'll be here."

"Oh. What's going on?"

I close the distance between us and grab her hands. "You know I can't tell you."

Laney waves a hand dismissively. "Yeah, yeah. I know."

"I'll call either way, I promise." It's not always easy to accomplish, but so far, I've managed to find an excuse so my brothers aren't suspicious.

I make my way to the bedroom door and lean close to it to listen for sounds to indicate Shiloh is awake. When I hear none, I look over my shoulder and wink at Laney.

"Love you."

"I love you too."

And with that, I disappear down the hall and out the front door. As I walk to my own house, near the front of the compound, I think about the day ahead. What I didn't tell Laney is that I have to take care of one of the club's drug runners. He's been short on cash twice now, and that's twice too many.

When I reach my front porch, I see a single headlight coming over the hill. I watch as the Harley gets closer, and that's when I see it's Duck, the club's Vice President. He stops a few feet away from me but leaves the engine running.

"Are you seriously just getting in?" I ask.

"No, I ran out to get some milk," he responds sarcastically. "Jesus, of course I'm just getting in. Hard to peel myself away from a warm and willing body."

"One of these days, Duck, your prowling ways are gonna catch up with you."

He shrugs. "They can sure try." He eyes me up and down. "Now, care to tell me who you spent the night with?"

"What makes you think I spent the night with anyone?"

"Oh, I don't know. Could be the fact that you're wearing the same clothes as you were yesterday. Or the fact that you're standing out here with a grin on your face like some teenage boy who just banged his math teacher."

Same clothes? How the hell can he tell? I wear jeans and a T-shirt all the time, along with my cut.

"You caught me." I force a chuckle. "Spent the night with one of the club whores."

"But not at your house?"

I can tell he doesn't believe me, but I forge ahead anyway.

"Yes, at my house. I walked her back to the clubhouse where her car was parked."

"Uh huh," he says, with a tone that screams 'liar, liar, pants on fire'.

"Shit, grow up dude. I don't have to share my sexual conquests with you. Some of us prefer a little discretion."

"You do realize that everyone here doesn't give the slightest fuck about *discretion*." The word falls off his tongue like it's bitter tasting.

"Oh, no? What about Snow and Toga? They don't talk about what goes on in the bedroom."

"Yeah, they do. Maybe not as much as they used to, but they're married to ol' ladies. They don't count."

"Whatever." I'm tired of trying to keep the lie up. I turn

toward my steps and say over my shoulder, "I'm gonna try to catch a few hours of sleep before church. I'll see you there."

I open my door but before I can cross the threshold, Duck's words stop me in my tracks.

"Someday you're going to come clean about who you're seeing. And I, for one, can't wait to hear all about it. It's gotta be someone epic for you to be so secretive all the time."

I listen as he revs the engine and peels away, leaving me to wonder what he knows.

Nothing.

Duck knows nothing. And neither does anyone else. Laney and I have worked very hard to keep our secret.

I keep telling myself that until an hour later, when I finally drift off to sleep... alone.

CHAPTER 2
LANEY

"These came for you. Thought I'd bring them over."

I take the flowers from my brother's hand and carry them to the kitchen. Snow follows me and sits on one of the stools at the island. He remains silent while I arrange the lilies in a vase and set them on the counter.

"Who are they from?"

Magic.

I lift the card from the center and open it. It reads 'from your secret admirer', as it always does when Magic sends me flowers. It's his way of circumventing any questions and protecting our relationship.

"I guess I have a secret admirer," I tell my brother.

"What?"

I bury my nose in the flowers and sniff, loving the smell. "What do you mean 'what'?"

Snow rises from the stool and begins to pace the room. "This is the third time in two months that you've gotten flowers from a secret admirer. I don't fucking like it."

"And I don't fucking care."

I shift to the end of the counter, lean against it, and cross my arms over my chest. Snow gives me a look that always makes me want to slap it off of his face. That look that says he doesn't approve, that he's judging me and finding me faulty in some way. One of these days, I am going to slap it off, and I'll take an immense amount of pleasure from it.

"Laney, you don't know who this guy is. It could be some creep, or worse yet, someone who is trying to get to the club through you."

Indignation rolls through me. "Seriously? It would be worse if they were trying to get to the club than a creep? So what does that mean, exactly? That if they showed up on my doorstep and forced themselves into my home and raped me, it would be okay as long as they don't come at the club?"

"That's not what I meant, and you know it."

I take a deep breath to calm myself. What Snow doesn't know is that I *know* who the flowers are from. And he's neither a creep nor out to get the club. He's one of them and—

"I'll have someone posted outside every night, just in case."

My heart rate spikes, panic setting in. If I have a guard outside, I won't be able to see Magic. No. No, no, no.

"That won't be necessary."

Snow closes the distance between us and bends to be at eye level with me. "If you think for one second that I'm going to sit back and do nothing when there could be real danger out there, you've lost your goddamn mind." His face reddens. He's angry. I suspect more at himself than at me. "I made that mistake once, and I'll be damned if I make it again."

"I don't want anyone posted outside my house," I argue. "I'm a big girl and can take care of myself."

"But you shouldn't have to. I'm here to protect you."

"Zeke," I begin. Using his given name usually tells him I'm serious. "I don't need nor want your protection. Why can't you respect that?"

His face falls, and he hangs his head. "Because the last time you dated, it was someone I brought into your life, and ended up ordering his death because he hurt you and Shiloh. What if this—"

"I know who sent the flowers." The words are out of my mouth before I can stop them.

Snow's head whips up, and he scowls. "Why wouldn't you just tell me that?"

Because it's Magic. Because I don't want him to die like Cedric did. Because, because, because.

"If I told you I was dating someone, I knew how you'd react." I eye him up and down. "And you're proving my point."

Snow's shoulders deflate, and he leans elbows on the counter. "Am I ever going to get it right with you?"

I step up to my brother and rest my head on his shoulder, suddenly feeling guilty for my reactions to him. "It's not that you get it wrong, Zeke. It's just..." I heave a sigh. "You take it too far is all."

Snow straightens and wraps his arms around me in a hug. "You know it's only because I love you, right?"

"Yeah, I—"

"Uncle Zeke!"

We both turn toward the front door in time to see Shiloh barrel through it and race toward us. My brother bends down to lift Shiloh when he launches himself at him.

"Shiloh, my man. Long time, no see."

Shiloh laughs. "You just saw me at your house."

"I did?"

"Duh. It was like, not even an hour ago."

Snow smacks his head like he just remembered. "That's right." He sets Shiloh on his feet and looks toward the door. "Where are Aunt Sami and Lennox?"

"At home." He rolls his eyes when Snow bristles. "Don't worry, they watched me from the porch."

"Well, you never can be—"

"Too careful," Shiloh finishes. "Yeah, yeah, I know."

"See," I say. "Even he feels the weight of your *protection*."

"Hey, my man," Snow says as he crouches down to Shiloh's level. "Why don't you go play in your room for a few minutes while I talk to your mom?"

Shiloh lifts his eyes to me. "Can I go outside and play?"

"Sure," I tell him, ignoring my brother's imploring stare.

Shiloh races out the back door while Snow rises to his full height and continues to glare. Before he can get a word out, I hold up a hand.

"Spare me the lecture," I tell him. "You've dedicated your life to this club and to making sure our compound is the safest place we can be." Tired of arguing with him, I let my shoulders sag. "Trust yourself, Zeke. I'm safe here. We're safe here. Certainly safe enough for a little boy to play in his own backyard."

Snow glances out the window over the kitchen sink, and I follow his gaze. Shiloh is running around shaking a stick at some invisible opponent. My heart expands at my son's ability to create his own little world and be perfectly content in it. I refuse to take that away from him.

"Listen, Laney," Snow begins. "I'll do my best to back off, but that's not going to stop my worrying about you." He

24

tips his head toward the window. "Or him. Or anyone else under my protection. But you also have to give a little. Try to understand where I'm coming from."

"I do," I insist. "But that promise to our parents was made years ago. And when they asked you to take care of me, I don't think they meant for you to stop me from having a life. Besides, you've done a great job. I turned out pretty well, I think. And that's because of you. Remember that."

He shoves a hand through his hair and sighs. "Fine. Just promise me one thing."

"What's that?"

"If you need me, you won't let your stubborn pride get in the way."

"I promise."

Snow nods and shifts to start walking toward the front door. "I better get home and check in with Sami before Church." He looks over his shoulder at me. "Do you want her and Lennox to come over and stay here tonight, while we're out on our run?"

"She can if she wants to, but we'll be fine."

He looks as if he wants to argue, but he wisely does not. He nods again and walks out the door. When he's gone, I go out the back door and sit on the patio to watch Shiloh play.

Content settles over me at the almost mundaneness of it all. The only thing missing is Magic. With him sitting beside me, both of us watching Shiloh without fear of being found out... that is all I need to complete my picture of the perfect life.

CHAPTER 3
MAGIC

The sniveling pleads only make me more determined to inflict untold amounts of pain on the man rolled in a ball in front of me. My lips tug into a sinister grin as I think about it. He can shout and scream and beg all he wants. We're in the custom shed situated in the woods at the back of the club compound, and there's not a soul on the planet that can hear him. No one other than me, and I love the sound.

"Pl-please," he begs.

"Save it," I bark. "Not even God can save you now."

"I didn't—"

My boot connects with his gut, and he howls in pain. I barely even know this guy, but it doesn't matter. He shouldn't have kept the profits of his drug slinging, at least not the amount he owed the club.

He wraps his arms around his stomach, as if that will ease the pain, when the only thing it does is open him up to other attacks.

Fucking idiot.

"I know you weren't about to try and make excuses," I snap.

"They're not excuses, bro."

Yep, total fucking idiot.

I bend down and clutch his throat. He claws at my hand, gasps for air, and just as he starts to go limp, I shove him away from me, onto the concrete floor.

"I'm not your bro," I seethe. "I'm your judge, jury, and executioner."

That's not entirely true. The club is his jury, Snow his judge... but I *am* the fucking executioner.

"Call Snow, he'll tell ya," he tries. "It was a loan."

This time, I can't stop the laugh that bubbles up from my gut. I throw my head back and let it out. It's always funny to me the lengths people will go to, the lies they'll tell, to get out of death. Well, I don't work that way. Maybe they could make a deal with the devil and cheat death for a while, but I'm not the devil. I'm the man the devil himself fears.

"Who the fuck do you think ordered me to kill you?" I ask once I've sobered.

"B-but, he's met me, he knows my little boy, my wife. He couldn't possibly want me—"

"This isn't a hostage negotiation," I snap just before my boot connects with his head. "Giving me details about your life isn't going to save you."

He falls to his back, clutching his face, as if that will somehow make the blood and pain disappear. Newsflash, it won't.

"Besides, we know all about your family," I tell him. "They'll be fine. The club will make sure she's financially compensated for the first year. And if, after that, they can't make a go of it, there's a shelter downtown where they'll always have a bed." I rest my hands on my hips and look down at him. "We're not monsters, ya know?"

But to him, we are. Or, more accurately, I am. And I'm okay with that. I welcome it even. That's the only way to keep our employees in check. With fear. And to ensure that fear, there has to be action.

"Anything you'd like me to tell them?" I ask, giving him a courtesy he doesn't deserve.

I do this with all my victims. It's the one part of my job that I don't like. Hearing what they think passes as heartfelt emotion. It makes them human when I need more than anything else to only see them as the trash they are. Begging is better. Much better.

"Tell..." He tries to drag in a breath. "Tell them that I... I didn't do this."

I whip my gun out of the holster I wear at my back and lean over to press the barrel against his forehead.

"You really want your last words to them to be a lie?"

He shrugs but says nothing. Rage boils under my skin. He's giving up. The begging has stopped, the crying has slowed. He's finally accepted his fate, which makes this a whole lot less satisfying.

I holster my gun and then grab the knife I keep tucked in my boot. I toss it in my hand a few times before bringing it to his chin, the tip of the blade nicking the skin.

"Giving up so easily?" I taunt, twisting the knife in my hand so it drills a hole into his flesh. "That's a pussy's game."

He reaches for the handle, and just as he closes his fist around it, I use that moment to yank the blade away, causing it to slice through his palm. He hisses in pain as blood trails down his hand, over his fingers, and drips onto the floor.

I stand and walk to the side where there's a chair. The steel legs grate across the ground as I drag it toward the center of the room. Once it's situated where I want it, I return my attention to the weakling on the floor.

"Get up," I demand.

His eyes widen, but he makes no move to do as he's told. I reach for his bicep to yank him up, but he pulls away.

"Wrong move, motherfucker." Or the exact right move to make this better for me. I step behind him and haul him to his feet by gripping him under his armpits. I shove him into the chair and shift so I'm in front of him again. "There, isn't that better?"

My mind flashes back to another man, another chair, another day in paradise. That man I tied up and walked away while he burned. This one, well, he's not going anywhere, and it'll be fun to watch him burn while trying to escape. Watch that one last ditch effort to save himself.

"I asked you a goddamn question!" I shout, pissed that he's quiet enough for my mind to wander.

He nods.

"Use your words."

I lift my knife and bring it down to pierce through his arm. He howls in agony, and his nodding becomes more frantic.

"Y-yes, it's better."

Freeing the blade, I walk around behind the chair and stop when I'm on the other side of him. I lift my hand again and thrust it through this arm, grinning when his howls become longer, more pain filled.

"Wh-what do you w-want from me?"

I tilt my head. "Oh, nothing much." I move to stand in front of him again. "Just to make you suffer."

I spend the next twenty minutes doing just that. I carve

the man up like a kid carves a pumpkin on Halloween. The only thing missing when I'm done with him is the gooey pile of seeds at his feet.

Blood coats the floor of the shed, the puddle spreading with each passing second. My heartbeat thunders in my ears, drowning out the man's shallow, barely-there breaths. How he's still alive, I have no idea, but he won't be for long.

I retreat toward the door, admiring my handwork as I do. Precise cuts and in a deceptively chaotic pattern over his torso, covering his arms and legs like bright red ribbons. It's... perfection.

Satisfied with my night's work, I push open the steel door and step out into the fresh air. After taking a few deep breaths to clear the copper stench from my nostrils, I turn and bring down the wooden latch to barricade the man inside.

Stepping back from the shed, I admire the structure Snow had built two years ago. It's become like a second home to me. Inside, it's a torture chamber, my office, so to speak. But on the outside, it looks like every other ramshackle shed a hunter may stumble across in his travels.

Worn wood, designed to look weathered by the elements, wraps the steel torture vault, allowing it to blend into the trees like a chameleon. The inside is fully fireproof, with a drop floor that leads to the pits, as we call them. Essentially, whatever doesn't burn, goes into the pits, thereby leaving no evidence.

I reach up to pull on the single piece of wood that sticks out at the corner of the structure, as if the wind had done some damage. I can't hear the whoosh of fire my action ignites inside, but I can watch from the tiny opening in the door, the one that looks like it's simply a knot in the wood.

Bright, searing hot flames finish my victim off. I was hoping he'd try to escape, which certainly would have made this a spectacular show, but I suppose I got a little carried away with the up close and personal side of his demise.

When the flames start to die down, I shift to the tree where I hung my cut. I didn't see any reason for it to get blood stains on it. After putting it on, I start walking back toward the main area of the compound. I don't worry about what remains in the shed because the floor will open on its own once the sensors are triggered by a preset temperature drop.

The closer I get, the more sounds of normalcy reach me. I try to quiet my mind, to put the last hour or two behind me, but it's difficult. I live for what I just did. Well, that and the day I can tell the world about Laney.

But for now, that shed is where I relieve all my anger and frustration at the circumstances of our relationship. It's where I can shout my indiscretions to the rooftops and no one but the dead person walking can hear me.

The shed is where I can be one hundred percent me, no matter how vile or lovesick I am.

CHAPTER 4

LANEY

Rolling onto my side, I groan when I see it's still dark out and Magic's side of the bed remains empty. I tried to stay awake and wait for him but dozed off sometime after two in the morning.

I throw the covers off my body and swing my legs over the edge of the mattress. Making my way through the house, I turn off the few lights I left on for him, convinced he's not going to show. When I reach the kitchen, the clock on the microwave reads four twenty-three. Yeah, he's definitely not coming.

On the way back to my bedroom, I peak into Shiloh's room and assure myself he's still safe and sound in his bed. It's a habit that I haven't been able to break since the night Magic killed Cedric, not that I want to break it. I'm his Mom, and it's what moms do.

As I'm climbing back into bed, my phone dings from its perch on my nightstand. I lift it to see the notification of a text from Magic.

Sorry I didn't make it over. Rough night. I'll see you at the clubhouse later. Love you.

I smile at the message. I'm used to these 'rough nights'. I'll ask him about it later when I see him. and he won't tell me anything. As he shouldn't. The last thing we need is for him to blab club business to me and the other brothers finding out. It's better this way, safer. But asking him about it makes things feel... normal.

Try to get some sleep. Love u too.

I return my phone to the nightstand and slide under the blanket. Closing my eyes, I pretend that Magic is next to me, curled around my body, shielding me from the real world and keeping me in a cocoon.

I manage to fall back asleep but am next woken up by the bed shaking uncontrollably. Shiloh's giggles trickle through my sleep-fogged brain. I've asked him many times to not wake me up by jumping on my bed, but when I hear how happy he is, I don't have the heart to scold him.

"Isn't someone full of energy this morning?"

After rubbing the sleep from my eyes, I reach out and latch onto Shiloh's legs and pull them from under him. He bounces on the mattress, laughing the entire time.

"Mo-om," he singsongs.

"Shi-loh," I mock.

I drag him down to sit next to me and wrap my arm around his shoulders.

"You hungry?"

"Starving," Shiloh says.

"How do pancakes sound?"

"With syrup?" Shiloh licks his lips.

"All the syrup you can handle."

My son scrambles to his feet and races to the door, his fist in the air, yelling, "Yay!"

Before following him out to the kitchen, I step into my bathroom to grab my robe and put it on. I traipse from the room and find Shiloh already pulling out the mixing bowl and skillet.

We work together to make breakfast and one hell of a mess. Shiloh devours his pancakes in minutes, along with half a bottle of syrup.

"Go take a shower, Shi," I instruct him as I clean up our dishes.

"But I'm just gonna get dirty when I play later," he complains.

"Shi, don't argue with me. Go get a shower."

He hangs his head but doesn't argue. As he turns the corner to walk down the hall, there's a knock at the door. I rush to answer it, praying it's Magic and knowing it's likely not.

"Hey, Laney," Sami greets me.

"What's up?" I ask, stepping aside so she can enter.

"Oh, nothing much." She sits on the couch and grins at me. "Other than I hear someone has a secret."

My muscles tense. "A secret?"

"Don't play dumb with me." Sami pats the cushion next to her, and I reluctantly sit. "Snow told me all about it."

My head whips up. "Snow knows?"

My stomach churns and my heart pounds.

Sami narrows her eyes at me, confusion wrinkling her forehead. "Of course he does. He said you told him all about it."

Of course I didn't tell him. Why would I tell him about Magic and tip that domino over?

"I just can't believe you didn't tell me you were dating. And that this mystery man sends you flowers."

Oh, right. That.

"Well, I..." I shrug. "You know how it is when you're in a new relationship," I lie. "I just wanted to see how things went before I introduced him to everyone."

"Makes sense, I guess. Tell me one thing though."

"What?"

She leans in like this is some sort of top-secret discussion. "How is he in bed?"

I can't stop the chuckle that escapes. This is the sort of thing girlfriends talk about, and quite frankly, I miss it.

"Best I ever had," I reply honestly.

Sami swats my arm. "I knew it. Here we all are thinking you've taken some ridiculous vow of celibacy but you're really getting freaky with your man."

"A vow of celibacy?"

"Well, you know, since Cedric." I arch a brow, curious how she knows about him, and she waves a hand dismissively. "Snow told me all about what he and his sister, Marlene, did to you both." Sami shakes her head. "Thank God for Magic, right?"

"What's Magic have to do with it?" I ask, wondering where she's going with this.

"He's the one who took out Cedric, right? That's what Snow told me."

"Well, isn't my brother full of secrets to spill?" I half-joke.

"Hardly. The only reason I know about them is because Marlene sent some odd letters, and I happened to open them."

"Really?" My curiosity is piqued. He's never told me about any letters.

"Oh yeah," she confirms. "She made some vague threats about getting revenge and yada, yada, yada. Snow assures me there's nothing to worry about."

Of course he does. He thinks he can take on the world and will do anything possible to protect those he loves.

"Anyway, back to your love life," she says before I'm forced to respond to the bombshell she just dropped. "So, best you ever had, huh?"

Thoughts ping-pong around in my brain, trying to keep up with her back-and-forth conversation.

"By far the best."

"Dammit," she quips. "I guess I owe Fallon a hundred bucks."

"For what?"

"Because she's the only one who thought you were in some secret relationship. I tried to tell her that you wouldn't keep something that juicy from us, and you damn sure wouldn't be able to keep it from Snow, but I was wrong."

"Fallon knew I was dating?"

Sami shrugs. "She suspected." Her face lights up. "And get this."

"What?" I ask, frustration building that my love life is the talk of the club.

"You'll never guess who she thinks you were seeing."

My blood runs cold.

"Who?"

"It's ridiculous really," Sami says rather than answer the question. "You're too smart for—"

"Who does she think I'm dating, Sami?"

"She thought…" She laughs, barely able to get the name out. "Shit, she thought it was Magic."

Well, fuck.

CHAPTER 5
MAGIC

S moke rings rise through the air as I make little 'O's with my lips after puffing on a Marlboro Red. The music bumps in the background, and the dancing has already begun. If you could call it dancing. It's more like vertical fucking, but who am I to judge?

The party started only a few minutes ago, and it's taking everything in me not to stare at the door, watching, waiting for Laney to enter. I made that mistake once and got caught by Duck. Fortunately, he was hammered, and it was easy to convince him I was waiting for one of the club whores, but I took a lot of ribbing after that. So much so that it made me uncomfortable because Laney would have to hear it.

"Yo, Magic!"

Speak of the devil. I shift my gaze to Duck, who's surrounded by three woman and sporting a stupid grin.

"You're not seriously going to sit at the bar all night, are ya?" he asks me, his voice booming to be heard over the music.

I lift the cigarette I'm holding, as if that explains everything.

"Fucker, you can smoke and dance at the same time. Hell, I bet you can fuck and smoke at the same time."

"I'll be there in a minute," I assure him, annoyed that he's not dropping it. "Hey, have your prowling ways come knocking yet?" I ask to shift the attention to him.

"Ha-ha, very funny."

I force a laugh and stub out my cigarette. Turning to face the bar, I smack the smooth wood to get the attention of Little Man, the prospect who's bartending tonight.

"What can I get ya?"

"A beer and a shot of Jack Daniels."

"Comin' right up."

Just as he sets the shot in front of me, I feel it, feel her. I swivel to face the doorway and see Laney standing there with Heather, one of the employees at a shelter in town that the club provides protection from.

Laney's eyes shift over the crowd until they land on me, and her smile lights up the room. Heather's eyes, on the other hand, land on Duck and a scowl graces her face.

"Oh shit," I mumble. "Looks like prowling ways are knocking hard."

"Huh?" Little Man asks as he slides a beer toward me.

"Nothing." I chuckle. "But keep an eye on Duck tonight. It's shaping up to be a good show."

Heather stomps toward Duck, and when she reaches him, she grabs his bicep to spin him around. His eyes widen when he sees who it is. What I wouldn't give to be a fly on his shoulder right now.

Great show or not, I'd much rather focus on the beauty weaving through the crowd toward me. Laney's wearing jeans and a bright green halter top, which pushes her tits up into mounds of flesh I want nothing more than to bury my face in.

Get a grip. Now isn't the time or place.

"Hey, Magic," she says when she reaches me. She hops up onto a bar stool and tells Little Man what she wants. When he walks toward the alcohol stash Snow keeps for the ladies, she leans in close to me. "We've got a problem."

"I know." I nod toward Duck, who's now in a full-blown argument with Heather, if his flying hand gestures are any indication. "He's fucked, isn't he?"

Laney follows my gaze and then shakes her head. "Yeah, I'm not talking about them."

I whip my head to face her. "What?"

Little Man sets a glass of wine and a shot of Tequila in front of her before walking to the other end of the bar. Laney downs the shot quickly.

"Fallon knows about us," she hisses as she slams her glass upside down on the bar.

Fear knots my muscles.

"What? How?"

"I don't know." Laney's face falls. "We've been so fucking careful, but I guess she's suspected for a while."

My muscles loosen the slightest bit. "So she only suspects?"

"Well, yes, but still. This isn't good."

"No, no it's not. But we can deal with suspicion."

Laney's eyes narrow and her lips pinch together. "Did you know there was a bet about my love life going on?"

I arch a brow. "Seriously?"

She takes a sip of her wine and bliss crosses her features as she swallows. "Shit, remind me to thank Snow again for stocking only the best for us."

"Laney, focus," I snap, needing to hear about this bet.

"Right." She shakes her head. "Anyway, there was a bet that I'd taken some sort of celibacy vow. Apparently, Fallon was the only one who thought I was actually getting some, and she thinks, or thought, that it was with you."

"Huh."

I can't stop the grin that spreads at the thought of Laney and me in bed. Both of us naked and our arms and legs tangled beneath the sheets, our bodies slick with sweat, my tongue—

Laney slaps my arm and not in a playful manner.

"Now who needs to focus?" she grits out.

"Sorry."

She waves away my apology. "It's fine. But I need you to put on a good show tonight. I had to tell Snow this morning that I was dating someone. He doesn't know who, but he's bound to be paying more attention now. And we have to dispel any rumors that it could possibly be you."

"Jesus, Laney." I run a hand through my hair. "You know I hate flirting with anyone else."

"Yes, well, we don't have a choice."

"There's always a—"

"Magic."

I roll my eyes before twisting to look at Minnie, the club whore currently running her gaudy red nails down my arm.

"Hey, Minnie," I force out, trying to inject even the slightest bit of excitement into my voice.

"Care to dance with me?"

Laney practically shoves me into Minnie's arms. "He'd love to."

I shoot Laney a glare before allowing Minnie to drag me into the sea of others already dancing. Don't get me wrong, Minnie's good looking, in a 'rode hard and put up wet' kinda way. And her legs might as well remain in an open position because if there's a body with a cock, she's doing her best to straddle it. Hell, I think I'm the only dick in the place she hasn't taken a joy ride on.

"How have you been?" she asks me, trying to initiate conversation I couldn't care less about.

"Fine."

Minnie flattens her palms on my chest and winks. "You certainly feel fine to me."

I grab her hands with the intention of pulling them away from my body, but she only twists them to lock her fingers in mine.

"Mmm, Magic, I have a feeling this is gonna shape up to be a great night."

She steps closer, too close. Her boobs press against me, and she grinds her pelvis. When my cock doesn't stir, she leans back and gives me a questioning look. I don't know what she wants from me. She's never going to turn me on, not like she's expecting. My dick only salutes to one woman, and it most definitely isn't Minnie.

As she does her best to turn me on, my eyes find Laney, who's now in the middle of the dance floor with Heather. Duck is nowhere around so Heather must have properly put him in his place.

Laney must sense my stare because she locks eyes with me, and there's no mistaking the hurt flashing in hers at the scene she's taking in. My instinct is to shove Minnie away from me and go straight to Laney to assure her she's the only woman I want, but I ignore it. Laney asked me to put on a show and that's exactly what I'm doing. Or trying to at least.

Minnie's hands shift from my torso to the button on my jeans. It takes a moment for it to register that her fingers have found their way into my boxer briefs.

Fuck, what is she trying to do? Tickle me into arousal?

I grab Minnie's wrist and yank her hand out of my pants. "Minnie, stop." My little show be damned.

"Oh, but you know you like it," she teases.

Irrational anger slams into me. "Is that what you were feeling?" I bark. "Because if it was, I think your 'fuck me' meter needs a tune up."

Minnie pokes out her bottom lip and tears well in her eyes. That might get to some, but not to me. I've seen her do it too many times to my brothers, all of whom fall for it. Or at least their peckers do.

"Don't," I grate out. "The fake emotion doesn't do it for me either."

Her face immediately reddens. Ah, I've touched a nerve... unlike her. Minnie stiffens her spine and squares her shoulders.

"Fine. Go home alone tonight," she says with a bite to her tone. "See if I care."

She stomps off, and I can't help but feel anything but relief. I know I need to make the others think I'm enjoying any woman who comes my way, but it's wrong. So damn wrong.

"Yo, Magic, what's wrong with you?"

Snow's voice penetrates through the music, and I twist to look at him.

"What do you mean?"

"Minnie was all over you, and for what? A tongue lashing?" He arches a brow. "And not the good kind."

"Stuff it, Prez." I start toward the bar, and he follows. "I'm just not feeling it tonight."

"You haven't been feeling it in months," he counters. "There was a time you'd celebrate your victories in the shed." He claps a hand on my shoulder. "What's up?"

42

Oh, nothing. I'm just a one-woman man and that woman is your sister.

"Nothing's up," I insist. "Shit, why are you and Duck so concerned about my sex life?"

"Bro, we don't give a damn about your sex life, but we do give a damn about you."

"Yeah, well, I'm fine."

"Good." Snow lifts his hand to get Little Man's attention. He orders both of us a shot before sitting on a stool. "Listen, I need a favor."

"Sure, Prez, anything."

He looks over his shoulder, his eyes darting toward his sister and then back again. "It's Laney."

"Oh?"

"She told me that she's seeing someone but wouldn't tell me who."

"I hate to break it to you, but she's a grown ass woman. She can date whoever she wants."

"I know." Snow heaves a sigh. "But I worry about her, you know that?"

"Yeah, I know." I take the stool next to his, curiosity settling in. "So, what's this favor?"

"I need someone to watch over Laney, make sure she's okay." I open my mouth to speak, but he holds up a hand to stop me. "I know what you're going to say. That she's not going to be happy about it or that I should trust her more. That's just it, Magic, I *do* trust her. It's whoever the fuck she's seeing that I don't trust."

And you probably shouldn't, considering that person is lying through his teeth to you.

"And what am I supposed to tell her when she realizes I'm hanging around on your orders?"

I tell myself to not argue with him, to take the orders

and be grateful that I can legitimately spend more time with Laney, but the words come out anyway.

"I don't know. You'll figure something out."

Yeah, the truth.

"Fine, but don't be surprised when she figures it out. She's not stupid, ya know?"

"No shit. But…" Snow lowers his head for a moment before lifting it to lock eyes with me. "Listen, I've got reason to be worried."

Immediately, the hair on the back of my neck stands on end. "Why?"

"Remember Marlene?"

"How could I forget her?"

"She's been sending letters, threatening revenge or some shit. I've promised Sami that there's nothing to worry about, but I'm not so sure."

"Why haven't you brought this up in church?"

Snow glares at me for daring to question him. "Keep in mind who you're talking to," he barks. "I have my reasons."

"No disrespect meant, Prez, but you're telling me now so you must have a reason for that too."

"Look, I don't really think anything will come of these threats, but I can't be in two places at once. I have Sami and Lennox at home, and I have to make them my priority. But I can't leave Laney and Shiloh vulnerable either. That's where you come in."

I know I shouldn't look a gift horse in the mouth, but I'm riding a fine line between simply obeying and being giddy for having Laney and I thrust together.

"Why don't you just tell your sister the truth? She's not exactly some fragile female who can't handle herself."

"Like she handled herself with Cedric?"

I bristle at the name and the insinuation that Laney did

something wrong back then. It's on the tip of my tongue to remind him that he invited Cedric into his sister's and nephew's lives, but I manage to keep myself in check.

"That was three years ago. She's grown a lot since then."

"Of course she has," Snow agrees. "But she's always going to be my responsibility."

"Don't let her hear you say that."

"Too late."

"I figured."

"Well, you wouldn't have been able to keep your mouth shut either if you'd seen the flowers she got, the look on her face when she read the card."

"Flowers?"

My mind flashes to the last time I had flowers sent to Laney. It was about a month ago. I remember so well because we'd argued the night before, and the lilies initiated an incredible round of make-up sex.

"Yeah, they were delivered yesterday morning, and I—"

"Yesterday?"

"That's what I said."

I didn't send flowers yesterday. What. The. Fuck?

"She had this expression on her face that told me everything I needed to know. Of course, when I questioned her about it, she denied that it was anything, but eventually, she caved. Said she was dating someone."

"You sure it was yesterday?"

"Fuck, Magic, keep up," he snaps. "The day doesn't matter. She's dating someone, and I don't know who the bastard is."

Thank God for small favors.

"Add in this bullshit from Marlene, and I'm losing my mind."

Same, brother.

"So, you'll keep an eye on her, right?"

You bet your ass I will. My eyes and every other part of me.

"Of course I will," I say instead of voicing what's really on my mind.

"Thanks, Magic," Snow says. "I knew I could count on you."

He stands and looks over the crowd. When his eyes land on the door, he frowns.

"Looks like your night is about to come to an end." He slaps me on the back. "Laney's leaving early."

I shift my gaze to follow his and see the door shut behind Laney.

"I'm on it, Prez."

CHAPTER 6

LANEY

The breeze sends goosebumps spreading over my skin as I walk back home from the clubhouse, each one a pinprick to the annoyance that forced me to leave the party. Seeing Minnie stick her hand down Magic's pants almost did me in, but I managed to keep myself together.

Then everything went sideways. Magic stopped her and ended up spending the next twenty minutes talking to Snow. No doubt about me, if the men's poorly hidden looks in my direction are any indication.

Assholes.

"Laney, wait up!"

I look over my shoulder and see Magic coming after me, but I don't slow down. His legs are much longer than mine. If he really wants to catch up, he can. Apparently, he really wanted to.

Magic's fingers wrap around my forearm, halting my steps. I turn to face him and glare.

"Why are you running from me?" he asks before I can get a word out.

"I'm not."

"Bullshit," he barks.

"What do you want, Magic? I'm tired and just want to go home."

"Bullshit." He drops my arm. "What the hell is wrong? What happened?"

The genuine concern in his tone almost quiets my frustration... almost. That's the thing about Magic. He loves me in a way that allows him to quickly bury whatever else is on his mind so he can focus solely on me. I love him just as much, but I haven't quite mastered that ability.

"Nothing happened," I snap, yanking out of his grip, my anger building with each passing second. "And therein lies the problem, doesn't it?"

"What are you talking about?" he asks, confused.

"Why did you push Minnie away?"

"Are you serious?"

It isn't lost on me that most women in relationships would be grateful to have a boyfriend who doesn't tolerate when another chick touches him. But I'm not most women. I'm me and he's Magic and we aren't supposed to be together.

"I asked you to do one simple thing, and—"

"One simple thing?" he seethes. "One simple fucking thing? Do you have any idea how *not* simple it is to pretend to be interested in someone else? I highly doubt it because I'm the one always having to do the pretending. Club whores, party guests, waitresses, goddamn women walking down the street... I am always putting on a show. And it tears a piece of my soul out every single time."

My anger deflates like a popped balloon, and my shoulders sag. When he puts it like that...

"I'm sorry," I say quietly.

Magic glances around us, no doubt making sure there's no one lingering, and then he brushes a stand of hair out of my face. He holds the back of my head and pulls me toward him so I can bury my face in his chest.

"Me too," he says. "But dammit, Laney, I hate this. I feel like a teenager sneaking around so my parents don't find out I'm dating a girl they don't approve of. It feels a lot like we're ashamed of what we're doing."

I lean back and lift my eyes to his. "I know. But we have to keep up pretenses. You know what would happen if—"

"Yeah, I know. I'm just not sure how much I care anymore. Consequences be damned, I want people to know that you're mine."

Taking a step back, I brace a hand on his chest. "And they will. When the time is right." Before he can start debating on when that will be, I invite him inside.

"Can you stay tonight?" I ask as I grab us both a beer out of the refrigerator.

"Tonight, and tomorrow and the day after that."

"Ah, so you're who my brother assigned to protect me?"

"Yep."

When I hand him the beer, I expect him to follow me into the living room to sit down, but instead, he steps up to the island.

"Why didn't you say anything?" he asks, his stare practically burning a hole into the flowers he sent.

"I wanted to thank you, but—"

"Where's the card?"

Confused, I pull the card from the drawer where I keep all the others and hold it up for him to see. "Right here."

He snatches it out of my hand and skims it, his face hardening as he does. Why is he mad? Did they get the card wrong?

"The lilies are beautiful. Thank—"

"I didn't send them." He slaps the card down onto the counter.

"What?"

He finally turns to face me, and his eyes are blazing with fury. "You heard me, Laney. I didn't send the flowers."

"But..."

"Snow thinks your secret boyfriend sent them."

"I had to tell him *something*," I insist. "He was talking about putting a twenty-four-seven watch on me and Shiloh. I had to stop that."

Magic raises a brow and sticks a hand out like he's going to shake mine. "Hi, I'm Magic. Your twenty-four-seven watch."

I slap his hand away. "Okay, okay, I get it. It doesn't matter what I tell him, he's going to do what he wants."

"Right. And he's worried that the flowers have something to do with the letters he's been receiving from Marlene."

"How do you know about those?"

"He told me tonight, when he was asking me to keep an eye on you and Shiloh."

I run a shaky hand through my hair. Surely this has nothing to do with Marlene. I shudder at the thought because if Marlene is involved, then so is Cedric.

No. Not possible. Cedric is dead.

"This is a nightmare," I grumble, rather than giving voice to my fears. If I don't acknowledge them out loud, they can't really be a possibility.

"Look, I'm here, and as long as that's the case, nothing bad is going to happen. First thing tomorrow, we'll start trying to figure out who the flowers really came from.

Surely the shop where they were ordered can tell us something."

"Okay." I nod. "Yes, okay. And what about tonight?"

Magic grins but his face quickly falls. "Where's Shiloh?"

"He's at Snow's house with Lennox. Carnie is watching them until Snow and Sami get back from the party."

"Carnie?" He arches a brow.

"Yeah, he's great with the boys. Besides, you know how much they love hearing about his time as a carnival doctor. Between that and all the junk food he'll let them eat, they're in heaven."

His grin returns. "Then tonight, I'll take you to heaven too."

"Oh?"

"But the dirty, adult heaven," he clarifies, as if I needed it. "Not the teeth rotting heaven."

I throw my head back and laugh. When I sober, I kick start our trip by standing on my tiptoes and fusing my lips to his.

Heaven, indeed.

CHAPTER 7
MAGIC

"You have to tell them."

Snow glares at me as the others file into the room. He watches as each member takes their standard seat. Once everyone is sitting, Snow focuses on me.

"Sit down Magic," he commands.

"Prez, c'mon, you know I'm right."

"Sit. Down."

I move to the only empty chair in the room and sit. Crossing my arms over my chest, I lean back and wonder if my request even matters.

Duck stands up, and he and Snow begin our motto.

"What the patch binds together, let no force tear apart. Satan's Legacy now and forever."

This is how we begin every church session. We've all pledged our lives to the club, to our brothers, and we make a point to honor that. As we should. And it always ends the same, with a lot of table pounding and foot stomping. In other words, loud.

"Shut the fuck up." Duck shouts to be heard, and the room slowly quiets. "That's better."

"Thanks, Duck," Snow says before nodding to his Vice President to sit down. "I've got some new business to discuss today, but before we do that, let's go through our usual order of business." He turns toward the club's treasurer. "Spark, how are our finances looking?"

"Great, Prez," Spark replies as he flips through the pile of papers in front of him. Spark doesn't trust computers, so all of his work is done the old-fashioned way. "I sent cash to Georgie's wife and kid, so they're set for a year." He holds a hand up. "And before you ask, yes, I made sure it was anonymous and untraceable back to us."

"Even with that loss, and the profits Georgie kept from us, we're still in the black?" Snow asks.

"Absolutely. Fallon's non-profit, Source of Love, is raking in the donations, so we're no longer supporting that endeavor. The shelters we provide protection for are paying on time, and all of our drug runners, now that Magic took care of Georgie, are also on time." Spark glances at me. "Seems word travels fast."

"If that changes, let me know," I tell him. "I have no problem taking care of anyone else who steps out of line."

"Of course you don't," Toga comments. "You thrive on that shit."

"Damn right."

"Okay, okay. We all know Magic is fucked up," Snow says in an attempt to regain control of the conversation. He turns to Duck. "How are things going at the shelters?"

Duck averts his gaze for a split second before he answers. "Things are good. No problems lately."

"And how's Heather?" Carnie, the club doc asks, a teasing quality in his tone. "I heard things didn't go so well with her last night."

"She's fine," Duck snaps.

"Uh huh," Toga chimes in. "Dude, you're in love with the chick. Have been for a while. Why can't you just admit it?"

"Because love is for suckers and fools."

"Oh please, love is nothing to be afraid of." All eyes turn to me, and I want to call the words back. "I mean, Snow and Toga found love and neither one of them is a sucker or fool."

"Right," Toga says with a wink.

"What?"

Toga shakes his head. "Nothing, it's just that..." He glances around the room before settling back on me. "Well, if Fallon's to be believed, you're in love with someone."

"Yeah, I heard. The problem with her theory is she thinks that someone is Laney." I chuckle, hoping they buy my lies. "How stupid do you think I am?"

"What's wrong with Laney?" Snow demands.

"Nothing," I insist. "Nothing is wrong with her. Jesus, she's off limits, Prez. We all know that."

"So you don't deny that you are in love with someone?" Toga presses. Damn Fallon and her theories.

"Are we here for church or a gossip session?" I counter. "Because if it's all the same to you, I'd like to get on with business."

"Me thinks he doth protest too much," Duck says, completely botching his attempt at mimicking some classic he thinks he knows.

"No, no. Magic is right." Snow's tone is calmer. "Back to club business." He crosses his arms over his chest. "Anything routine we still need to talk about."

There's a chorus of 'no's and a flurry of shaking heads.

"Then I've got some new business." Snow takes a deep breath and blows it out. "Marlene is back."

"What?!" Carnie shoots up from his chair. "What's that crazy bitch want?"

I roll my eyes at his statement. For Carnie to call someone crazy, he must really have a low opinion of them because that fucker is certifiable. Let's just say, I'm glad he's on my side.

"I don't know," Snow admits. He pulls some papers out of his cut and sets them on the table. Duck grabs them and starts to read while Snow continues. "She's sent a few letters where she promises revenge. For what, I'm not sure. It could be for the way I kicked her to the curb, or because we killed her brother."

"*I* killed her brother," I clarify. "And there's no way it was traced back to us. Not only did I make sure of it, but we would have had authorities beating down our door if it had been."

"Agreed. But…" Snow runs his hand over his beard. "It doesn't really surprise me that she thinks the club is responsible."

"Well, I can tell you that she isn't the one who sent the flowers to Laney," I say.

"What flowers?" Brady, a patched member asks.

"Of course she didn't," Snow says. "The man Laney is dating did."

"Hold up," Duck says, lifting a hand. "What the hell are you two talking about?"

Fuck, that's right. They didn't know any of this.

Snow heaves a sigh and looks at me with censure in his eyes. "Laney's been dating again but won't tell me who. Apparently, this guy sends her flowers and shit." His forehead creases. "Magic, why would you think they were sent by anyone other than this mystery man?"

Fuck, fuck, fuck.

I shrug. "Seems odd to me that these flowers are showing up the same time as the letters. Figured it was worth checking into."

"And you checked into it?"

"Prez, you asked me to keep an eye on your sister and nephew. Of course I checked into it. I had to be sure. I called the flower shop this morning and all they could tell me was that it was a man who sent the flowers." *A man, but not the one she's dating.* "If Laney says they were from a boyfriend, the evidence points to that."

"I guess."

Snow doesn't look like he's completely buying my story. And I'm glad he's not. Whoever sent the flowers is up to no good. It needs to be checked into further. I just can't say that without drawing suspicion.

"It still begs the question, who the fuck is she dating? Until I know that, I'm not convinced Laney and Shiloh aren't in some sort of danger." He turns toward our road captain. "Dip, get in touch with your contacts and see what you can find out. I want to know for sure that this new boyfriend is no one to worry about."

"Prez, you already have me watching her, and needless to say, she's not thrilled about it. Do you really think digging deeper is wise?"

I feel like I'm on a seesaw. One minute, I want the club to dig deeper so we can get to the bottom of this and take out the threat. Then the next, I'm praying Snow will let it go because I don't want to be exposed.

I debate on coming clean, right here and now, but decide against it. I can't, not without talking to Laney first. This will affect her too.

"Do you really think I give a damn about what she

wants?" Snow barks before his shoulders slump. "Shit. I didn't mean that."

Yeah, you did. At least on some level.

"You're right, of course," I finally say, swallowing hard. "Her and Shiloh's safety needs to be a priority."

"I'm doing this for her own good," Snow insists. If I'm not mistaken, he's trying to convince himself, because he knows this will blow up in his face, one way or another.

It's going to blow up in your face too.

"Prez, I'll question some people, see what I can find out," Dip says, bringing the conversation back around to the task at hand. "I'll also see what I can find out about Marlene. If she's around, my contacts will know."

"Thanks." Snow claps his hands as if everything is solved. "Any other business?"

"Don't you think this is enough for one day?" Duck says with a laugh. "Or is there more you're keeping from us?"

"Watch it Duck," Snow growls. "I'm still the president of Satan's Legacy, and if I keep something to myself, I do it with good reason." He shifts his gaze around the room, practically daring anyone else to speak up. "If there's nothing else, we're adjourned."

Snow walks to the door and opens it, dismissing us all. When I start past him, he grabs my arm and holds me back. Once the room is empty but for the two of us, he scrubs a hand over his beard and sighs.

"So, how pissed was she last night?"

"What?"

"That you were on watch," he clarifies.

"Oh, right." I release a breath and shrug. "You know Laney. She wasn't happy about it, but she eventually calmed down."

Once I fucked her silly.

"Good, that's good." His forehead wrinkles. "What did you think I meant?"

"What do you mean?"

"Bro, did you smoke a joint before church or what? You're acting fucking paranoid."

I shake my head, silently chastising myself for being so weird. "No, no. Just tired."

"Yeah, sorry about that. Make sure you don't wear yourself out too much. Have someone take shifts during the day so you can get some sleep. I know staying up all night to do my bidding takes a toll. I appreciate it though."

"It's no problem, Prez, really."

"Well, thanks."

"Anytime."

Snow disappears through the door, leaving me there to try and regain my composure. What the fuck is wrong with me? I can kill a man without hesitating, but lying is tripping me up?

It's because of who you're lying to.

Unless I'm ready to pay for my sins, and subject Laney to some form of sanction as well, I need to get a grip. I've done well for the last year and a half. What's changed?

CHAPTER 8

LANEY

ONE MONTH LATER...

T flush the toilet and lean back against the tub in the hall bathroom. Sweat beads down my forehead, and I wipe it away with the wet washcloth I've had clutched in my hand for the last twenty minutes. My stomach muscles ache from dry heaving so much. I've been sick for three days now and have no idea why.

Maybe you're pregnant.

Ha! Impossible. Both Dr. King and Dr. Dryer told me so. When I was sixteen, during a routine pap smear, my gynecologist, Dr. King, found a cyst on my cervix that concerned her. A biopsy was completed, and, when the results were in, both Snow and I were called back to the office to meet with her.

At the time, Snow was my legal guardian because our parents had died. I was stuck with him when all I wanted was my mom. That's all any girl would want in a situation like that.

I don't remember much about that meeting, other than hearing the doctor say 'cervical cancer'. The rest is a blur. Or so I thought.

"Are you sure?" Zeke asks, leaning forward in his chair.

"I'm sorry, but yes, your sister has cancer."

Zeke lifts my hand and squeezes. He's always doing that, trying to comfort me in some way. Since our parents died a year ago, he's become my protector, my savior. And this will be no different.

"Laney, you have several options," Dr. King says. I lift my head to look at her, but all I see is a monster telling me my life is over. "I've made a referral to Dr. Dryer, our resident oncologist, and she'll go into more detail with you, but there are medicinal treatments, as well as surgical. It'll be up to you which you choose."

I shake my head, trying to make her disappear. Maybe if I shake it hard enough, I can propel the hands of time backward. Yes, I'll go back a year. My parents will still be here, I'll be healthy. All will be right in my world.

"Laney, honey," Zeke says. "Did you hear Dr. King?"

No, I didn't hear Dr. King. Because Dr. King doesn't exist. She's a figment of my imagination.

"Laney?"

"No!"

"Laney?"

Magic's face appears in front of mine, blurry at first, but after several seconds, his image clears.

"Magic?"

He lifts my hands from my lap and brings them to his lips. "Of course, Sweet Cheeks. Who else would it be?"

I shake my head, dislodging the rest of the memory I thought I'd forgotten. I chuckle, the sound coming out forced. "Nobody." Embarrassment floods my cheeks.

"Okay." He pushes sweaty hair out of my face. "Still sick, huh?"

I nod, not trusting my voice.

"Why don't you let me call Carnie? He can at least tell you if he thinks this is something we should worry about."

"No."

He's been begging me to call Carnie since the first time I threw up. And every time, I shoot the idea down. Carnie is a good doctor, and I trust him completely, but it's weird. He's a club member, like a brother to me. No way am I letting him perform an exam.

"Then I'm calling your doctor. I can't stand seeing you like this." Magic gives a sad smile. "Besides, your annual screening isn't for a couple more months. What if it's—"

"The cancer isn't back."

"I'm sure it's not, but why take the chance?"

I swat Magic away from me and try to stand up. When I sway, he grabs my shoulders to steady me. Once I'm able to stand on my own, he drops his arms.

"Magic, the cancer isn't back. It's just the flu. There's nothing a doctor can do for that."

"Laney, please," he pleads. "Call the doctor. If not for yourself, then for Shiloh... and me."

Damn him for bringing my son into this. If I weren't as concerned as he was, I wouldn't agree. But if I'm being honest, I know something isn't right. Not that I'm going to admit that now. I just don't think it has anything to do with the cancer. Which means it's something else, some unknown beast waiting to take me out.

"Fine, I'll call."

THE PAPER that lines the table in Dr. Dryer's exam room crinkles as I shift. My oncologist was able to get me in right away, which scared me. When I called, I was immediately patched through to a nurse, who listened to my symptoms and proceeded to tell me to come straight to the office.

I wasn't expecting that. I thought for sure she'd tell me to call my regular doctor and drink plenty of fluids in the meantime. But no, that's not how it played out.

Worst case scenarios play over and over in my head, all culminating in my premature death. The door swings open, breaking through my mental planning of my funeral.

"Just tell me," I say before Dr. Dryer can even close the door. "I can handle it, whatever it is."

"Are you sure?" she asks, which only sends my fear up a notch, or ten.

Rather than answer, I wring my hands and nod.

"Well, then, Laney..." She takes a deep breath. "You're pregnant."

"I knew it. I mean, I was hoping it wasn't the canc—" I slam my lips shut and look at the doctor for the first time since she walked in. "What did you just say?"

Dr. Dryer chuckles. "You're pregnant." She peers at the paper in her hand. "Almost two months pregnant to be exact."

"But... you said... all my doctors told me..."

"Sometimes even doctors are wrong."

"Yes, but..." I swallow past the lump in my throat. Tears spring to my eyes, and I swipe at them. I don't know yet if they're happy tears or 'oh my God, what the fuck am I gonna do' tears. "All the radiation, all the treatment... I've had sex for years, and nothing ever came from it. I was told nothing ever would."

"No, Laney. You were told it was unlikely. And it was. *Very* unlikely. But it was always possible."

How could I have been so wrong? Oh God, what if I'd gotten pregnant by Cedric? I mean, I am the mother of his child, but I didn't give birth to Shiloh. It was supposed to be impossible.

"I take it this isn't good news," Dr. Dryer comments.

"No. Yes. I don't know." I give her a pained look, imploring her to tell me if it's good or bad.

"That's normal, Laney," she tells me, which is zero help to me. "And if I remember correctly, you were devastated when you were told you likely wouldn't conceive."

"I was," I admit. "Are you sure you did the test right? What does this mean for my annual screenings? Will the cancer come back? What if—"

"Whoa, slow down. One thing at a time." She sits down on her stool and wheels close to the table. "Yes, the test was done right. You're pregnant, no question about it. As for your annual screenings, this doesn't change anything. You'll still have them. Being pregnant does not cause cancer, so if it were to come back, it wouldn't be because of this."

"Good, that's good."

"Now, I have a question for you."

"Okay."

"While it's none of my business, and you can tell me so if you'd like, is the man in the waiting room the father? Because if he is, maybe we should have him come in here so we can tell him the news."

Fuck! Magic.

I forgot he was out there. He insisted on driving me to the doctor, in case I got nauseated again. We dropped Shiloh off with Sami so he could play with Lennox, then came straight here.

"Um..." I nod. "Yeah, he's the father."

"Do you want me to get him?"

"No!" The word comes out fast, sharp. "I mean, no, I'd like to tell him myself, if that's okay."

"That's perfectly fine," she assures me. "I have to tell you though, he seems like a keeper, if my nurses are to be believed. They tell me he's been pacing since the moment you were called back, demanding information every few minutes. He's worried about you."

Everything hits me all at once, and I let the tears fly. I'm pregnant with Magic's child. What should be a very happy thing is tarnished by what this means for his position in the club. I want to experience all of this with him, but how? I love him too much to put him through the hell he'll have to pay.

But he's the father.

I force a smile, sniffling to stop my crying. It shouldn't surprise me that my life is turning out the way it is. It's been one thing after another, a series of gut punches designed to knock me down. I always get back up though. And I will this time... eventually.

"He is a keeper," I finally say to the doctor, resignation in my tone. "The best man there is."

Which is exactly why I can't keep him.

CHAPTER 9

MAGIC

I tighten my grip on the steering wheel of my truck. I drove this because I didn't want Laney yacking off the back of my Harley, but I miss the sound of the wind. It'd be better than the silence.

Laney has been so quiet since she came out of the doctor's office. I've tried to ask her questions, but she dodges them all. Worry cascades over me like a waterfall spills over the side of a mountain. Cool, wet, never-ending.

"Would you mind stopping at Snow's house so I can get Shiloh?" she asks when we go through the gate and crest the hill at the compound entrance.

"Of course not."

"Thanks."

The exchange is forced, almost frigid. At least that's how it seems to me. I'm used to passion from Laney, not indifference.

"Are you dying?" I spit out, unable to bear all the horrible possibilities racing through my mind.

I glance at Laney as I shift the truck into park in front of

Snow's house and see a tear spill onto her cheek. She's smiling, but it's a sad smile, a broken smile.

"No, Magic, I'm not dying."

I blow out a breath, one scenario down and about a million more to go.

"Okay, then what is it?" I reach across the cab and lift her hand. She doesn't pull away, which is a step in the right direction. "Laney, I need to know. I'm..." I scrub my free hand over my face. "Fuck, I'm scared."

"Me too."

"Whatever it is, we'll get through it... together." I squeeze her hand in a gesture of reassurance, but I don't know if I'm doing it for her or me. Probably a little bit of both.

Laney shakes her head. "I'm not so sure."

"I am. We're a team, you and me. And I'm here for whatever it is."

She yanks her hand from my grip and twists so she's facing the window. "That's just it, Magic. I don't think we can be a team for this."

If I thought I was scared and worried before, that has nothing on the terror her words inflict. Rather than respond, I pull out my cell phone and bring up Snow's contact information so I can text him.

Me: Would u mind keeping Shiloh a little longer?

I know he's home because his Harley is parked by the steps. I just hope he hasn't seen us sitting out here in the truck. When I see a curtain on one of the front windows shift, I know my hope was in vain.

Snow: Yeah, but ur already here. What's wrong?

Me: Nothing's wrong. Laney's still feeling a little under the weather.

Snow: Okay. If ur sure that's all it is. I'll bring him home in the am so she can get a good night's sleep tonight.

Me: Thanks

I toss my phone onto the seat and shift the truck into gear.

"Where are we going?" she asks without looking at me.

"Home. Shiloh's spending the night with your brother."

"That's probably for the best. I could use some alone time to process everything."

"Alone time my ass," I snap, frustrated beyond belief that she's shutting me out like this. "I did this so we could talk. You're gonna tell me what the hell is going on."

When I park in front of her house and cut the engine, Laney finally looks at me. "Magic, please don't do this. Can't we just have one more day where I can pretend everything is as it should be?"

"No. And that right there is why." I throw my hands up in the air. "Laney, this is ridiculous. There is nothing so bad that you can't tell me. And there's certainly nothing that you could tell me that will make me walk."

Laney opens her door, and after jumping down to the ground, she looks over her shoulder at me. "I know that. You're a good man, Magic. Too good."

She closes the passenger door and trudges up her porch steps. I hop out of the truck and reach her side as she's unlocking the door. I follow her inside but remain in the living room while she goes to the kitchen.

I watch as she pulls out two waters from the fridge and thank her when she hands one to me. The cold liquid glides down my throat, cooling me from the inside out, but it doesn't detract from the emotions coursing through me.

Laney paces for a few minutes, her face etched with uncertainty, and when I can't take the silence any longer, I close the distance between us and grab her biceps to stop her in her tracks.

"This is ridi—"

"I think we—"

We both laugh, but it sounds uncomfortable.

"Go ahead," I tell her when she makes no move to speak again.

Her eyes lock onto mine, and it hits me. The quiet resolve I see in her irises is like a knife to the heart. I'm not going to like what she has to say. Laney tries to gain control and urges me toward the couch, but I resist.

"Just spit it out, Laney."

She swipes her forehead and then wraps her arms around herself, as if that will protect her from my reaction to whatever shit she's about to spew.

"Magic, I think…" She pauses to take a deep breath. Just as her face starts to turn red, she forces the air back out. "I hate this."

Laney moves to the couch and plops down. She pulls a pillow into her lap and holds on to it like her life depends on its closeness. As much as I want to march out of here and pretend she's not about to say what I think she is, I can't do it. My legs won't listen to the command.

She lifts her eyes to mine, and a sheen of tears well up. The need to comfort her is strong, and of course that's the action I can follow through on. I sit down next to her and put an arm around her shoulder.

She buries her face in my side as sobs wrack her body. I stroke her hair, whisper that it will be okay, everything I always do when she's having a bad day. Gone is the fear that she's ending our relationship, the thoughts of her dying. The only thought in my head now is to protect her from whatever is causing her sadness.

After several minutes, she lifts her head and wipes her nose on her sleeve. Her eyes are bloodshot, her face splotchy, and yet, she's still the sexiest woman I know. She leans forward and presses a kiss to my lips. It's short, brief, and feels... different somehow.

Laney takes a deep breath. "I'm pregnant," she says on an exhale.

That isn't at all what I thought she was going to say.

"Pregnant?"

She nods.

"That's not possible."

"That's what I thought too."

"But the cancer, the treatments..."

"I know."

The information slowly sinks in and settles like a ton of bricks. It's good news, the best really. I want a family with Laney. She's it for me. But something tells me I'm not it for her, no matter how much she wants it to be so.

"I'm gonna be a dad," I whisper, still reeling. "We're having a baby."

Laney nods. She's doing a lot of that lately.

"I know this forces us to come clean to everyone, but I'm fine with that," I tell her, excitement building. Sure, I'm not thrilled that I'll likely be voted out of the club, but in the long run, it won't matter. I'll have her and Shiloh and our child. "I'll talk with Snow tonight. I'm sure that'll mean

69

church in the morning, but after that, we can start looking for a place—"

"Magic, stop."

"Listen, I know this isn't how we wanted this to happen, but we don't really have a choice anymore."

"Yeah, we do… there's always a choice."

"Okay, maybe until you start to show, but this isn't exactly something that we can keep hidden." I rest my hand on her still flat abdomen.

"Magic." She brushes my hand aside and stands. "*We* aren't going to do anything. I will tell Snow about the baby. But I'm not telling him you're the father."

"Excuse me?"

"You are the best thing that's ever happened to me, Magic." When I stand, she tries to grab my hands, but I shift away. "I love you, so fucking much, and that's why I have to do this." Laney lowers her head before rolling her neck and looking back at me. "Your first reaction is to go tell everything to Snow, and I get it. But I can't let you do that. You'll be voted out, Magic, don't you get that?"

"And you think I give a fuck?!"

"Maybe not right this second, but someday? Yeah, I think you will. And then what? We get married and raise Shiloh and our child?" She shakes her head. "No, that can't happen. Because you'll no longer be a part of Satan's Legacy and you'll be full of resentment. I can't do that to you. I won't do that to you, and I certainly won't do it to our kid."

"Do what, Laney?" I shout. "How is marrying me and us being a family worse than cutting me out of my kid's life?"

"Because this way, you'll be able to still be a part of it all. At least on some level. You'll still be around."

"Oh, so I'll be the fun uncle, watching from afar as some

other man swoops in and takes what's mine? I don't fucking think so."

"Magic, please, try to see reason. What if the club votes to do worse than kick you out? What if they vote to kill you? You know as well as I do that that's a possibility. If that happens, you won't be part of anyone's lives."

"That won't happen," I insist.

"But you don't know for sure, do you? You can't promise me that my own brother won't have your death ordered, just like he did with Cedric. Can you?"

No, I can't. And therein lies the problem. Everything she says makes sense. I don't like it. I'm furious, in fact. But I know Laney. Unless I can promise her that everything will be okay, she's not going to budge.

Well, neither am I. One way or another, I'm going to keep what's mine. I'm going to make this right. I will be a father to my child and to Shiloh. And a damn good one. I will be a great husband and prove to her that she's wrong.

But even I know it's not going to happen right this minute. I have to talk to Snow. Man to man, brother to brother. And I just have to pray to a God I don't believe in that it goes better than I deserve.

I look Laney in the eye. "Fine. If this is what you want, I'll walk away. But I won't stay away, Laney. I can't."

"Yes, Magic, you can. You don't have a choice."

She walks to the door and opens it before stepping to the side and silently telling me to leave. I cross the threshold but stop just outside the door and turn to her.

"There's always a choice."

CHAPTER 10
LANEY

My vision blurs as the taillights of Magic's truck turn into dim red blobs. My knees threaten to buckle, so I tighten my grip on the door, as if that will keep me upright.

What have you done?

When I can no longer see the truck, I step back and close the door. Without the support, the energy it takes to stay upright is too great, and I collapse to the floor. Pain radiates through my wrists and up my arms when I try to catch myself. But it doesn't compare to the agony piercing my heart.

"Motherfucker," I groan, just as the tears break free and cover my cheeks.

I scoot and rest my back against the door and let them fall. There's no use trying to stop the emotions whipping at me like pelting rain in a hurricane. I pull my knees to my chest and wrap my arms around them, as if that will protect me from any damage. Logically, I know it won't, but I have to try. If I do nothing, I'll break.

I have no idea how long I sit on the floor, but when the

MAGIC'S TORMENT

sobs subside, I feel exactly like I did before they started. They weren't cleansing, or cathartic, or anything else a good cry is supposed to be. No, they simply got reabsorbed by my skin and sent straight back to my heart, where the pain has intensified.

"Pull yourself together," I mumble.

I manage to get to my feet, only swaying slightly until I'm as confident as I can be that I won't fall right back on my ass. I shift to the couch and sit, pulling a pillow into my lap. Immediately, I'm hit with Magic's scent. I breathe it in, inhaling deeply, and try to keep it in my nostrils. Unfortunately, if I don't want to pass out, exhaling is a must. Bringing the pillow to my face, I inhale the smell several more times before throwing it across the room.

"Goddammit!" I scream.

I grab the other pillow on the couch and scream into it, as loud as I can, hoping that will cleanse me in a way the tears couldn't. When my throat can no longer bear my breakdown, I heave a sigh.

"What the hell have you done, Laney? You're fucking pregnant." I rest my hand on my stomach. "You're having Magic's baby, and you just broke up with him. Way to go."

The longer I sit there and think about the events of the day, the more anger replaces regret. I did what I had to do to protect the man I love. My decisions weren't about me nor my happiness. I'd do well to remember that.

With that in mind, I make another decision. I can't keep this from Snow, as much as I'd like to. But knowing Magic the way I do, he's not going to wait long before he tries to be the hero. I've got news for him... it's my turn.

I walk to the island in the kitchen where I set my purse when Magic and I returned from the doctor and dig inside it until I find my cell phone. Just as I'm about to hit the speed dial for Snow, the device rings and 'unknown' pops up on the screen.

I tap the answer icon.

"Hello."

Silence.

"Hello?" I repeat, thinking that maybe there's a bad connection.

Still, no answer. But I do hear someone, they're breathing coming through the line it loud and clear. It's heavy, weighted in a way that has the hair on my arms standing up.

"Who's there?"

The breathing intensifies, speeds up. Mixed in are quiet moans, and bile rises up the back of my throat when I imagine what they're doing.

"Who the fuck is this? Is this some sort of sick joke?" Nothing changes. "Get a life," I snap and then end the call.

I toss my cell back into my purse. I don't have time for this shit. I've got a list of real-life problems to handle, and prank phone calls are not on it.

Shiloh is still at my brother's, so I decide to walk there instead. Maybe fresh air will do me some good. I grab my house key and lock up behind me.

As I walk, my heart rate picks up. I have no idea how Snow is going to respond when I tell him I'm pregnant. Probably similarly to how I did when the doctor told me. He heard the same prognosis I did for all those years: it's not possible.

Add in the fact that I have to pretend that my fake boyfriend is the father, and this should turn out well.

Yeah, about as well as the black plague did for all the people it wiped out.

I round the corner and freeze. Magic's truck is parked in

front of Snow's house. It's sitting there, taunting me. Of course he came straight here. Why couldn't he just listen to me? I don't think for one second that I'm going to get lucky and this is just a friendly social visit. No, by now he's probably confessed everything, and Snow is circling the wagons... or Harley's in our case.

I break out into a run and take Snow's steps two at a time. I don't bother knocking. I used to never knock, but one time I walked in on my brother and Sami doing the nasty on the kitchen counter and manners became a common thing for me. That's an image I can't unsee.

Magic and Snow are standing in the living room, facing each other. Magic's head whips toward me and his eyes narrow, as if I'm the one in the wrong here.

Seriously? He's pissed at me?

"Laney," Snow says. "Tell me he's wrong."

"I... well..." I don't exactly know what Magic's told him so I'm not sure how to answer. I glance around the room. "Where's Sami?"

"She went to the clubhouse to grab a drink with Fallon and a few of the other ol' ladies."

"And Shiloh? Where's he?"

Snow stares at me for a moment, almost as if he's trying to look through my questions to what's hovering just beneath them.

"He and Lennox are watching a movie in the bedroom."

"Oh." That's something, I guess.

"Ya done avoiding my question?"

"I'm not avoiding anything," I counter, and I can tell when his eyes narrow that he doesn't believe me.

"Are you pregnant?"

"Laney," Magic says before I can answer. "I'm sorry. I only—"

"Shut up, Magic," I snap. "I think you've said enough for one day."

"So it's true?" Snow asks. "You are pregnant?"

This isn't exactly how I wanted this to play out, but thanks to Magic, I'm going to have to come clean.

Damn him.

Finally, I nod.

Snow closes the distance between us and lifts me into a bear hug.

"That's amazing!" He spins me around before setting me on my feet. "I mean, we all thought... wow, I'm going to be an uncle again."

Confusion rolls over me. He's happy?

"Yeah, I know." I dart my eyes to Magic and back again. "So much for it being impossible."

Snow walks back to stand next to Magic and slings an arm around his shoulder. "Brother, I think a party is in order. My sister is going to have a baby."

Magic's gaze settles on me, but I can't read any emotion in it. "She sure is."

"Zeke," I begin and take a step in his direction. "You're okay with this?"

My brother looks between Magic and me before jostling Magic. "Of course I'm okay with this. I'm fucking excited." He tilts his head. "Aren't you?"

"Yes, I am, it's just..." I pull my bottom lip between my teeth, unsure how to proceed. "I just..."

"It's a shock, I know," Snow says. "But Laney, it's a baby. Remember how happy you were when Shiloh was put in your life? You're going to get to experience that all over again, but from the very beginning."

What sort of warped universe have I stepped into? This makes no sense. Snow should be livid, not stupid happy.

"And you're not upset with Magic?" I ask, tentatively.

"Magic? Why would I be upset with Magic?"

Again, I dart my eyes to Magic, silently begging him for help, even if I don't deserve it, and he gives an almost imperceptible shake of his head.

Oh my God. He didn't tell him everything.

Which means I've just opened up the door to Pandora's box and have to figure out how to shut it before all hell breaks loose.

"Laney?" my brother prods.

I wave my hand as if my reason for asking is silly. "No reason. I just figured you'd be upset that he knew before you."

Snow's eyes remain locked with mine and his hand falls from Magic's shoulder. "He's the one who took you to the doctor. It makes sense that he knew before me." He strokes his beard. "But that's not why you thought that, is it?"

My brother has always had the ability to ferret out my lies. I've gotten much better at keeping secrets over the years, out of necessity, but sometimes my efforts bomb.

"Of course it is," I insist.

"Okay, I'll concede that you're being honest about that, but you're keeping something from me." He glances toward Magic, who shrugs, and then back to me. "Did that fuck you were seeing run for the hills when you told him? I'll kill him."

I shake my head. "No, no, nothing like that. Quite the opposite, actually."

What the hell am I doing? Don't give him more info to work with.

"Good." Snow smiles. "When do I get to meet the man? Before the wedding, I hope," he chuckles.

I'm glad someone thinks this is funny.

"There isn't going to be a wedding, Zeke." Finally, something I can be honest about.

"I don't understand. You say you've been seeing this guy for a while, that you love each other, and now you're pregnant. Of course there's going to be a wedding."

I fold my hands in front of me and try not to fidget too much. "It's not that simple."

"Jesus, Laney. Now is not the time to be stubborn. Everyone knows you're capable of being a single mom. A great one too. But you don't have to be."

Snow walks to his kitchen and pulls two beers and a water out of the fridge. He tries to hand a beer to Magic, but he shakes his head. When he hands me the water, I take it, grateful for something to do with my hands.

"You always do this," Snow continues. "For once, can't you put aside your need to prove yourself to me and do what's best?"

My skin heats up at the anger that snakes through me. Of course my brother would make this about him. And I suppose, to a certain degree, it is. But not for the reasons he thinks.

I take a large gulp of the water before screwing the cap on the bottle. "That's not what I'm doing."

Magic shifts on his feet, something he does when he's uncomfortable.

"Prez, maybe you should take it easy on her," Magic suggests.

Snow keeps his eyes on me but responds to Magic. "This has nothing to do with you, so shut it."

"Right," Magic mumbles. "Nothing to do with me."

I pin my stare to Magic. What the fuck is he thinking?

Snow brings his beer bottle to his lips and takes a long

pull. Afterward, he sets the bottle on the coffee table and turns to Magic.

"What's that supposed to mean?"

Fuck, fuck, fuck.

"Nothing."

"No, not nothing. What the fuck are you two not telling me?"

In an effort to turn this conversation around, I step between the two of them and focus on Snow.

"Nothing. He's just pissed because he's my latest body-guard and now he's going to have to deal with an emotional pregnant woman instead of the normal badass I am."

Even I don't believe a word I just said.

"Bullshit."

"It's not bullshit," I cry.

"Laney, give it up," Magic says at the same time.

"One of you better tell me what the fuck is going on before I lose my shit."

I try to come up with something to say, some lie that Snow will believe, but I'm not fast enough. Magic opens his mouth and ensures that Pandora's box can never be closed again.

"I'm the father."

CHAPTER 11
MAGIC

I'm the father.
  I'm the father.
  I'm the father.

Snow's hands ball into fists at his side, and that's when I realize I said the words out loud.

"What did you just say?"

"Zeke, it's not—"

I hold up a hand to stop Laney's protest and she presses her lips together. The daggers shooting from her eyes appear freshly sharpened and no doubt would kill me if they were real.

"You heard me, Snow," I say, turning away from Laney to focus on her brother, my president.

Soon to be former president.

Snow's chest heaves with every breath he takes. He doesn't swing right away, which is what I remind myself when the upper cut to my jaw takes me by surprise.

"You motherfucker." Snow grabs me by my cut and yanks me toward him. "I thought I could trust you. When I asked you to keep an eye on her and Shiloh, I didn't mean for you to fuck her and ruin her life."

Before I can say anything, he continues.

"Dammit, what's she supposed to do now? No doubt this is why the boyfriend left. Doesn't want to raise another man's baby. You couldn't keep it in your pants, could you?"

"Zeke, you're misunderstanding." Laney steps up next to her brother, resignation in her eyes. "Or maybe you just don't want to admit what this all means. Magic is my boyfriend." Her face falls. "Or he *was*."

Snow doesn't acknowledge his sister in any way as he shifts a hand to my throat. "How long?"

"How long what?"

He squeezes. "How long have you been banging my sister and lying to me about it, lying to everyone about it?"

The pressure on my neck makes it difficult to respond without wheezing. "A while."

"How. Fucking. Long?"

"Almost two years."

Snow shoves me with all the force of a bear on steroids. I stumble backward but don't fall. He advances, fists up and ready. I do nothing to protect myself from his hatred. I deserve whatever he dishes out, and I'll take it with a smile on my face. Because once he's done, the rest of my life can go back to normal. Laney will be mine again.

He inflicts blow after blow, and blood covers my face, drips down onto my clothes. When he lifts his leg and kicks me in the stomach, I double over in pain. Yet, I still don't fight back.

"Zeke, stop it!" Laney shouts. "You're gonna kill him."

"Exactly," Snow seethes before bringing his knee up into my face.

I stumble backwards and try to recover, but it's useless.

Snow continues his assault, no holds barred. A few more well-placed kicks, and I crash to the floor, grazing the coffee table on the way down. My mind is starting to go hazy, Laney's pleas fading into the background.

He drops to his knees and continues to take his rage out on my face, my chest, anywhere he can hurt me. Unconsciousness hovers, but never takes me. I wish it would. I can handle the physical pain, but the thought of him hating me, of my family disowning me... it's unbearable.

Think about the good. Think about Laney, the baby, the life you will have.

My mind wanders as I picture the years we'll have together. This allows me to block out Snow's unchecked beating. The last image in my mind is of Laney and I sitting on a porch, both with gray hair and grandbabies playing in the yard.

"Get the fuck out of here."

The words yank me back to reality. I'm bathed in my own sticky blood, the metallic taste coating my mouth like a thick milkshake.

"Magic," Snow growls. "Get the fuck outta my sight before I forget that killing you needs to be put to a vote."

I BARELY RECOGNIZE the battered man looking back at me from the mirror. I'm no stranger to having my clock cleaned. You don't act as the enforcer for a one percenter MC without a few bumps and bruises along the way. But this kind of damage is a first because it was inflicted by one of my own.

My head is swimming in the booze I drank after practically crawling to my own place yesterday. My body sways as I try to focus on my reflection, but the only thing that keeps me steady is clutching the edge of the counter.

The light hurts my eyes, and the thought of what could happen at church hurts my soul. I should have known Snow would call an emergency session, but part of me had hoped it would be a few days.

I take a deep breath and square my shoulders. I shove down the urge to purge the alcohol and swat the light switch off as I leave the bathroom. I snag my cut off the chair as I make my way to the front door but stop short of exiting my house.

Glancing at my cut, memories flood my mind of the last ten years I've been a part of Satan's Legacy. Still images from my patching ceremony float in front of my eyes, only to be replaced by images of the numerous club runs, parties, prospects, club events, days in the torture vault in the woods, nights with Laney. Every single image is a memory that will stay with me forever.

I toss my cut back to the chair and leave without it. Might as well get used to not having it on because I'm not going to be a part of this brotherhood after today.

I ride my Harley to the clubhouse. I need the rumble beneath me, to feel the wind in my face as a Satan's Legacy brother one last time.

Walking into the clubhouse, my nerves are calmer than I expect. My head is too, considering how fucked up I was not five minutes ago. The main room is empty, and the only noise I hear is coming from the room where church is held. Snow did a good job clearing the place out.

Before entering church, I stand outside the door and take a few deep breaths. I know I have to go inside, but if I can put it off just a few minutes longer, maybe I'll—

"Get your lying ass in here, Magic." Snow's voice bellows through the door. "I can see your fucking shadow."

I grip the doorknob and twist it. When I walk into the space, I'm met with scowls, sneers, and glares. Everyone is already sitting down, other than Snow, and my normal chair is already occupied.

I move to stand next to Snow, as I know that's where the member on trial is supposed to be. On display for the others to judge. For the first time in years, I'm not the executioner. They are and this is the worst punishment a person can receive: threat of being ousted.

"What the patch binds together, let no force tear apart," Duck begins. He continues, with the other brothers in unison. "Satan's Legacy now and forever."

"As you all know, we're here because of information that was brought to my attention yesterday," Snow begins. "It pains me to be in this position and to see that Magic is the one standing here." He gestures at me. "But fuck if this isn't where we are."

"Looks like you started the party without the rest of us," Dip comments, referring to my many bruises. "Nice work, Prez."

"Shut up, Dip," Duck snaps. "This is serious."

"No shit," Dip retorts. "We're here because Magic has been lying to us for years. Not to mention he knocked up Laney who has been and always will be off limits."

"No disrespect, Prez," Brady, a patched member, says. "But Laney is a looker. Can you blame him?"

"And you kept putting them together by always assigning Magic as her personal guard," Carnie adds.

The more comments made, the more heat wafts off of Snow. I can feel his rigidity, his rage at being questioned. He brings both fists down on the table, rattling the few coffee mugs.

"That's enough!" he yells. The steam coming from his ears might as well be the whistling of a tea kettle because it's the only thing I hear in the shocked silence. "Despite what Dip and the rest of you seem to think, Laney and Magic being together is the least of my concerns."

Say what?

"That being said, I'll remind you that I'm the fucking president, and you don't get to question me." Snow turns to face me. "Magic, you lied. To all of us. And that won't be tolerated."

"Understood."

"What the fuck were you thinking?"

Is this a trick question?

No. It's not. He genuinely wants to know. And for that, he'll get a genuine answer.

"I was thinking that Laney is an amazing woman. I was thinking that I couldn't face another day without her as mine." I take a deep breath, ignoring the snickers coming from some of the others. "Prez, we tried to avoid each other, to ignore whatever there was between us. And we both failed."

Snow nods, as if he understands exactly what I'm talking about. And I suppose, to a degree, he does. Love isn't a foreign concept to him, especially since Sami and Lennox came barreling into his life. The only difference is he didn't even try to fight that connection. He simply brought them home and bam, they were his.

"Oh my God, Prez, he's a goner."

I glance at Toga, who also recently discovered love. If ever a woman was off limits, it would've been Fallon. She was Toga's former stepsister for fuck's sake. But that didn't stop him.

"Goner or not, the fact remains. He lied."

"So did Laney," Carnie points out. When Snow's face turns beet red, Carnie holds up a hand. "Now wait a minute. I'm not saying she should be punished, but Magic isn't alone in this. It takes two to tango. You brought us here to discuss his position in Satan's Legacy, and, to me, all the facts are important. He deserves that kind of consideration. It's a big deal to strip a man of his patch."

This is not going at all like I expected. And based on the pinched look on Snow's face, it's not going how he was hoping.

"Would you all listen to yourselves," Snow grits out from behind clenched teeth. "Magic has violated several bylaws." He shoots me a glare. "Not to mention he didn't even have the decency to show up wearing his cut."

"One-hundred-dollar fine is imposed for that infraction," Spark says, speaking up for the first time. "Magic, you'll have to pay that before the day is over. If you don't, a hundred dollars will be added with each subsequent day."

"Heard." I nod, grateful that the fine was imposed. It means I have a chance at remaining here, as a brother.

"Enough talk," Snow barks. "I'm going to pass out paper and pencils so we can vote. If you vote to keep Magic around, you must also write down what you think his sentence should be for lying." He slides a stack of paper and a pile of pencils to Duck. "Keep in mind that, per our bylaws, this is a silent vote. You talk, you walk. And on your way out, you can pay your fifty dollar fine to Spark for the infraction."

The next five minutes feel like an eternity. I'm being scrutinized, evaluated, voted on like some common low life. Yes, I lied. Had I known Snow wouldn't have been a dick older brother, maybe I wouldn't have. We'll never know.

"Time's up. Pass your votes to Duck please," Snow instructs.

Papers slide across the table, and Duck gathers them into a pile. He reads them for everyone to hear. At the end, the vote is two for stripping my patch and thirteen for keeping me around.

I heave a sigh of relief. I'm still a patched member of Satan's Legacy MC. In order for me to have been stripped of the patch, the vote had to be unanimous.

"Moving on to punishment," Snow says, pulling me back from my premature celebration.

Duck goes back through each slip of paper and reads the suggestions. I have to say, my brothers are nothing if not creative. The majority vote is for me to stay away from Laney for an amount of time to be determined by Snow, but those were mixed in with a month of gate duty, a week of prospect training, shaving my head, cutting off my dick, and an hour with Snow in the torture shed.

Snow shifts so he's facing me. "Magic, you will not be stripped of your patch, however, your sins are not forgiven or forgotten. You are sentenced to stay away from Laney for six months."

"Prez, she's pregnant. You can't expect me to stay away from her for the majority of that. It's my kid," I protest, frustrated with his cold-hearted sentence.

"Which is why I didn't make it a year." His face hardens. "You should be grateful. You'll still be able to be there for the birth, if that's what Laney wants. I suggest you take this time and think about how generous I'm being. Because if you get caught lying to the club again, about anything, there won't be a vote. You'll be stripped of your patch and sentenced to death."

I square my shoulders and bite my tongue. I want to yell at him about how unfair he's being, about how he's not only punishing me, but his sister as well. I want to drag his ass to the torture shed and give him a piece of my mind. I want, I want, I want...

"Understood," I say, also not wanting to poke the bear.

CHAPTER 12

LANEY

"Get a fucking life, asshole."

I toss my cell onto the couch cushion, and both Sami and Fallon stare at me like I've lost my mind.

"What?"

"Who the hell was that?" Sami asks.

I wave my hand dismissively. "Teenagers with no life. That's the fourth prank call I've gotten in the last week."

"Oh, God, I remember that phase," Fallon quips. "At the time, it was hilarious, but now that I'm grown, it's annoying as hell. If we ever get those kinda calls, I let Toga handle it. He's much scarier than I am." My face falls at the reminder that she has a man, and I don't. "Sorry, Laney, I didn't mean—"

"It's fine." I stand and walk to the kitchen. "Need another drink?" I ask them as I grab a water for myself out of the fridge.

"Nah, I'm good," Sami responds and looks at her phone. "It's already two in the morning, and I've gotta head home soon."

"I'll take one," Fallon says. "Tomorrow is my lazy day."

I snag the last remaining bottle of booze off my counter and a glass. I carry them to Fallon and set them on the coffee table in front of her.

"Might as well drink what you can, then. I need this shit out of my house."

The bottle has been tempting me since I learned of Magic's sanction. I know I can't drink it, but it's been hard because all I want to do is numb the pain.

"So, have you heard from Magic at all?" Sami asks.

Anger fights to break through. There was a time I wouldn't question why she's digging for information, but right now, I just don't know what her motives are. Is she asking as a friend, or as a mole for my twat of a brother?

"Not a word."

"That's probably for the best."

"The best for who?" I snap. "Me and his baby? Him?" I glare at her. "Or the best for Zeke? Because I'm not quite clear on that."

"Laney, I'm on your side with this," Sami says matter-of-factly. "Magic's punishment is extreme, but he has orders to stay away. You can't blame him for following them."

"Oh, no?" I begin to pace the living room. "Because rules and orders never stopped him from seeing me before. He broke every single rule he could just to be with me. And now that..." I take a deep breath. "All of a sudden, walking the straight and narrow is everything to him?" I shake my head. "I don't think so. He's a pussy and is using his punishment to put as much distance between us as possible."

"Is that what you think?" Fallon asks.

I throw my hands up in the air, so confused that my

brain is getting whiplash from my hormonal back and forth.

"I don't fucking know," I cry, tears welling in my eyes. "I'm pregnant and alone and the one person who should be here for me, who could make it all okay, isn't."

"Not because he doesn't want to be," Sami says.

I latch onto her words, ricocheting to the bright side. "What has he said? Have you talked to him? Does he—"

"Laney, stop," Sami demands in a tone she usually reserves for Lennox. "No, I haven't had a chance to talk to him. But this is Magic we're talking about. He's not a bad guy, and I doubt he's all of a sudden fallen out of love with you."

"She's right," Fallon agrees. "Magic's one of the best brothers in the club. And based on what you've told us, he's loved you with everything he has."

"Loved?"

"You know what I meant. A person doesn't just shut those feelings off. That's not how the heart works."

"Maybe you should try and talk to him," Sami suggests, surprising me. "What? I know I'm supposed to back Snow, but you're one of my best friends, and I hate seeing you like this. Maybe a few minutes with Magic will put your mind at ease."

I shake my head. "No, I can't. If he wants to talk to me, he'll find a way. I refuse to be the one to put him in a position he may not be able to get out of if the club found out."

"But—"

"I said no." I take a drink of water and then recap the bottle. "Look, I appreciate you both and am grateful for your advice, but I'm getting tired."

Fallon and Sami scramble to their feet.

"Of course. Sorry."

"No need to apologize," I assure them. "Maybe we can get together another night, continue this conversation."

While I'd love to hang out with them, I pray they understand that I really don't want to talk about Magic. Not now and likely not anytime soon. It hurts too much. I have to accept that I'm on my own, and apparently, Magic is too. The biggest difference is he doesn't seem to mind while I'm here feeling eviscerated.

"Yeah, another girls' night would be great," Fallon says. She glances at the bottle of booze still sitting on the coffee table. "Want me to take this?"

"Yes, please. Get the temptation outta here."

She grabs the bottle and tucks it under her arm. She and Sami make their way to the door.

"You know we love you, right?"

"That word is getting thrown around a lot lately." I force a smile. "But yes, I do. And I love you both too."

"Night."

"G'night."

They speak in unison before leaving. I lock the door behind them and make my way through the house to turn off the lights. I wasn't lying when I said I was getting tired. I'm exhausted.

I peek into Shiloh's room to check on him and see him sitting up in his bed.

"What's wrong?" I ask him as I flip on the light and then stride toward him. I sit on the mattress beside him and put an arm around his shoulders. "Can't sleep?"

Shiloh shakes his head. His little forehead wrinkles and he opens and closes his mouth several times, but no words come out.

"What is it?"

"Are you gonna have a baby?"

Well, shit. I guess the girls and I were being louder than I thought. I haven't told Shiloh yet about the baby because, even though it's confirmed, there's so much that still seems in the air.

I nod. "How do you feel about that?"

He shrugs. "A brother could be fun."

"And what if you have a sister?"

Shiloh wrinkles his nose. "That wouldn't be as much fun. I see how you and Uncle Zeke argue. No thanks."

Leave it to a little boy to oversimplify things.

"Oh, Shi, having a sister wouldn't be so bad. Yeah, Uncle Zeke and I have our moments, but I love having him as a big brother."

"Yeah, but does he love having you as a little sister?"

Um...

"That's a question you'll have to ask him."

"Okay. I will because I have to be prepared."

I chuckle for the first time tonight. I'm pregnant and feel like my life is going every which way but straight, and he just wants to be prepared if he has a sister. Ah, to be that young.

"Mom, can I ask you something?"

I kiss him on the head. "Of course you can."

"How come Magic hasn't been around lately?"

I stiffen for a split second before forcing myself to relax. "Why do you ask?" I'm not sure it matters why he's asking, but then again, his response can give me some insight into how *I* should answer.

"I don't know. I miss him, I guess. I like Magic."

"Yeah?" He nods. "Me too."

"So why isn't he around?"

"Well, Shi, Magic is very busy. Sometimes, what he does for the club keeps him away more than we'd like."

"It never used to."

No, no it didn't.

"Magic was always here. I know you didn't want me to know, but sometimes you guys played really loud."

Shit.

"Is Magic the baby's dad?"

"What?"

Shiloh heaves a sigh, you know, the kind reserved for when a child thinks his parent is the stupidest person on the planet. And who knows, maybe I am.

"Mo-om, I'm not dumb."

"I..." I clear my throat. "I never said you were."

"So just tell me. Is Magic the dad?"

"Before I answer that, maybe there are a few things we should talk about."

"I already know about where babies come from."

"Excuse me?"

I have not had the sex talk with my son. I figured I'd put it off until he was thirty. Or at least until he hit puberty and started showing an interest in girls.

He sighs again. "Uncle Zeke told me."

I'll kill him. My brother is a dead man.

"He did, huh?"

Shiloh nods. "So, is he?"

"Is who what?"

"Is Magic the dad?"

"Would that bug you if he is?"

"He is, isn't he?"

"Yes, Shi, he is."

Shiloh remains quiet for a moment, and then his face lights up.

"Cool. Magic will be a good dad." He looks at me with excitement. "Does this mean Magic will be my dad too?"

"Well, I, uh, I don't know."

Shiloh's face falls. "Oh. Did I do something wrong? Is that why Magic isn't coming around?"

"No, Shi, you did nothing wrong." My tone is soothing, reassuring. I hate that he feels like he's to blame for the circumstances when that couldn't be further from the truth.

"Then why isn't he here?"

"Well, Shiloh, that's a question for your Uncle Zeke. Why don't you ask him?"

There, take that brother.

CHAPTER 13
MAGIC

"We need to talk."

I stop in my tracks and turn around to see Snow standing at the edge of the tree line. I have a piece of shit waiting for me in the torture shed. I don't have time for one of Snow's 'talks' right now.

"Can it wait?"

He scowls at me. "No, it can't."

"Listen, Snow, I haven't seen Laney in two weeks. I've done nothing wrong. So if you don't mind, I'd like to—"

"This isn't about Laney," he snaps. "Well, not really." Snow reaches into his cut pocket and pulls out an envelope. He hands it to me. "Read this."

I open it and start to read the paper inside.

My dearest Snow,

I see you aren't taking me seriously. I've tried to make you see things from my point of view, tried to do things the easy way. But that means nothing to you. The only language you speak is 'hard way' so let's give that a try.

"What the fuck is this?"

"Marlene's latest. It came this morning."

I continue reading.

I know what you did, or more accurately, what you ordered. Maybe you should have ensured that everything was carried out to the letter. You see, fire is a funny thing. It doesn't always have the desired outcome. Fire, unlike, oh, guns, isn't a guaranteed finale.

The paper crinkles under my grip. What the fuck is she talking about?

I can hear your laughter now, as you think about it. Evidence, and even people, can survive a fire. Unless of course your torture chamber is used. That is definitely a step in the right direction for the club. Nice work there. Anyway, you'll see what I'm talking about... soon. I just hope that your loved ones can survive their intended demise like mine did.

Forever yours,
Marlene

"Magic, what does she mean her loved one survived?"

The unthinkable.

"She's just trying to scare you."

"Maybe, but what if she's not? She's basically telling us that Cedric didn't die. I thought you made sure he had?"

"I did." I think back to that night, that fire. It was the first time I'd used fire as a form of execution. Is it possible I made a mistake? "If there was anything to worry about, we'd have known by now."

My words sound false, even to my own ears. Not that

I'm lying, because I'm not. But I also don't know if what I'm saying is true.

"If I find out that you're lying, you'll wish your patch had been stripped."

"Prez, I'm not lying. I tied him up, set the fire, and left. The house went up in a blaze so fast I don't know how anyone could have gotten away."

"But it's not impossible, is it?"

Did I tie the knots tight enough? Was he more alert than I thought? Was Marlene around somewhere that she could have gotten him out?

"I guess it's not impossible, but…"

"But what?"

"It's highly unlikely."

"Unlikely? Un-fucking-likely?!" Snow begins to pace. "Unlikely doesn't fucking cut it."

"You're right," I concede. "It doesn't."

"You realize that if Cedric is alive, Laney is in danger. Not to mention Shiloh. What if those suspicious flowers were from him? And then there's the prank phone calls. You know as well as I do that flowers and phone calls won't be the goddamned end of it."

"And what am I supposed to do about it?" I snap, breaking under his pressure. "You ordered me to stay away, so I can't protect them, remember?"

"Oh, I remember. And that order still stands. But know this. If anything happens to either of them, or the baby, it's on you. It was your job to kill Cedric. And apparently, you failed at that. The blood will be on your hands, not mine."

With that, he storms away. I watch him walk back toward the main part of the compound, my heart heavy. He's right, if anything goes wrong, it'll be my fault. And that, more than anything else, is all the punishment I'll need.

I turn on my heel and walk the rest of the shed. I have so much aggression I need to get out that this guy is going to wish he had killed himself. I don't even remember what he did to deserve my wrath, but he's alive and breathing when he shouldn't be. That's enough.

I shove open the door and startle the man. He's sitting in the corner, but scrambles to his feet when he sees me.

"Look, Magic, I can explain." He lifts his hands, as if they could protect him.

Oh, right. His hands are what got him in trouble.

"This ought to be good." I take a few steps toward him, and he practically melts into the wall. "Go ahead. Give it your best shot."

"It's just..." He swallows hard. "I didn't know she was taken."

"She has a name."

His eyes widen, and his Adam's apple bobs. "Yes, of course, but..."

I tilt my head. "You don't know it, do you?"

"I... no, I don't remember."

I reach behind me and pull out my gun. I point it at him, not aiming at anything in particular. "Think harder," I spit out. "I'll give you three guesses."

"And if I guess wrong?"

Really? The gun isn't an indication?

"I guess you'll find out, won't you?"

The man takes a few deep breaths before spitting out the first name. "Sugar."

I pull the trigger and the bullet hits him in his right shoulder. "Guess again," I instruct over his screams of agony.

"Uh… um… Minnie."

Just how many women did he hit on?

Another bullet hits him in his left shoulder. My lips spread into a grin at his attempt to stop the bleeding of both wounds. Too bad for him, it hurts too bad to stretch that much.

"Guess again."

"Look, man, I don't know her name."

I pull the trigger again, aiming at his right kneecap. He collapses to the floor and blood pools beneath him.

"Jesus, okay, okay," he grumbles. He seems to think about it for a minute before his face lights up with recognition. "Laney! Her name is Laney."

I take out his left kneecap and then squeeze off another round into his stomach.

"What the fuck?" he cries. "Her name is Laney."

"It is," I confirm. "But Laney is mine." I shrug. "Hence the other bullets."

"Fine, fine. She's yours. I get it. I'm sorry. Now can you let me go?" His voice is weakened by the amount of blood loss. Good, it won't be long.

"Ah, ah, ah," I tsk. "Not so fast. One thing you should have bothered to learn, besides Laney's name, is how Satan's Legacy operates." I pull my leg back and deliver a swift kick to his stomach wound. "Ya see, when you enter this shed, you don't exit. At least not alive."

"But I sa—"

Blood splatters all over the wall behind him when the bullet pierces his skull. He slumps to the side, silent for the first time since I walked into this place. I check his pockets for any cash he may have, and finding none, I leave the shed.

Once I latch the door, I pull the lever to start the fire. I don't bother to watch through the knot hole. While every kill is satisfying, this one lacked the adrenaline rush, the euphoria I normally experience.

Damn Snow and his shit timing.

CHAPTER 14
LANEY

T hump, thump.
Thump, thump.
Thump, thump.

"It sounds so fast."

"Completely normal," Dr. Simons says as she holds the ultrasound wand pressed to my belly. "Your baby's heartbeat sounds perfect."

Sami, who came for moral support, squeezes my hand. "Hear that, Laney? Perfect."

"Have you thought about whether or not you want to know the sex of the baby?" Dr. Simons asks.

I nod, unable to speak past the ball of emotion in my throat. I shake Sami's hand because she and I discussed this on the way here and I need her to speak for me.

"She wants to know but not without the father," Sami responds. "She would like to get some printouts of the ultrasound if that's possible though."

"Of course." The doctor moves the wand and captures a few images. "How about this? I'll get you those pictures, and I'll also write down if it's a boy or girl and seal that in an envelope. When you and the father are ready, all you'll have to do is open it and find out."

"Th-that would be great," I choke out. "Thanks."

After Dr. Simons wipes the jelly off my stomach, she excuses herself, saying she's going to get everything ready so I can leave.

"Are you okay?" Sami asks when we're alone.

I wipe the few tears on my cheeks and take a deep breath. "Yeah, I'm fine. Just wish Magic was here."

"I know you do, hon. I imagine he wishes the same thing." Sympathy flashes in her eyes. "Have you tried to talk to him at all?"

"No," I admit, staring at my hands in my lap. "Even if I could, I wouldn't know what to say. He wrote me off the second Zeke declared we had to stay apart."

"Can I make a suggestion?"

I lift my eyes to her and nod.

"When we get home, why don't you ask your brother if he'll invite Magic over so you can give him the ultrasound pictures yourself?"

"You and I both know he won't agree to that."

Sami smiles. "I wouldn't be so sure. He and I have talked a lot. Well, I've done most of the talking and he's been forced to listen." She laughs. "I've been where you're at... pregnant and alone. Granted, Lennox's father was in my life, but he might as well not have been." Sami flaps her hand as if that doesn't matter. "Anyway, I think he's starting to understand just how much his rigid rules are hurting you, probably more than Magic."

Hope flares, but before I can ask any questions, Dr. Simons returns. She hands me two envelopes.

"One contains the images you requested. I printed two copies. One for you and one for Daddy. The other is the sex of the baby." I glance down and see 'Do not open until ready' on the smaller of the two envelopes. "Now, I want to see you back in two weeks. Dr. Dryer will be present for that appointment. Because yours is a high-risk pregnancy, we thought it best to coordinate your care as much as possible. Since we share a building, that makes it easier."

"Okay. Thank you."

"You're welcome. You can make your appointment on your way out." She turns to Sami. "It was nice meeting you. It's always great to see our patients having a solid support system."

"It was nice meeting you too. And trust me, Laney has a support system a mile wide." Sami chuckles. "Probably more than she'd like at times."

Dr. Simons finishes her goodbyes and exits the room. Sami and I walk out to the reception area, and I schedule an appointment for two weeks from today before we leave the building.

"You hungry?" Sami asks as we walk, arms linked, to her vehicle.

The downtown Denver street is busy, bustling with people either on their lunch break or enjoying the late summer sunshine before we're thrust headfirst into winter conditions.

"Starving." My shoulder is bumped, hard, by a man passing by and I turn to glare. "Watch where you're going, asshole."

The man looks over his shoulder, and my stomach bottoms out. My feet become glued to the pavement, bringing Sami to a halt along with me.

"What's wrong?"

I glance at her and by the time I look back to where the man was standing, he's gone. I shake my head.

"Nothing. I just thought I saw someone."

Cedric. You thought you saw Cedric.

Which is impossible because he's dead. Magic killed him three years ago. My pregnancy must be fucking with me, letting in fears I thought I'd overcome.

Cedric is dead. Cedric is dead.

I turn to Sami and smile. "Ya know what, I think I'd rather just go home. Maybe we can grab something at your place?"

"Yeah, sure."

We walk the rest of the block to where her car is parked. The ride home is quiet, the only sound coming from the radio. I hold onto my envelopes like my life depends on them remaining in my hands.

When we round the corner at the clubhouse, Sami and Snow's house come into view. Lennox and Shiloh are outside on the porch, eating hotdogs. The smell of the grill hits me when I step out of the car, and my stomach growls.

"Hey Mom," Shiloh calls out to me with a mouth full of food.

I walk to the porch. "Hey, Shi." I try to grab the last bite of his hotdog, but he yanks it out of my reach. "Aw, come on," I fake whine.

"I'm sure your brother made plenty. Why don't we go inside and see what's left?" Sami suggests, grabbing my hand and practically dragging me up the steps and through the door.

"Slow down," I laugh. "I'm not as fast as I used to be."

Snow is in the kitchen, standing in front of the stove, stirring what appears to be some sort of pasta.

"Oh my God, that smells so good." The scent of garlic invades my system, and my mouth waters.

"Good," Snow says. "Sami texted me that you two were

on your way. Figured I'd make you a proper lunch. Ya know, because of the baby and all."

"That's sweet," Sami says as she walks toward him and then rises onto her tiptoes to kiss him on the cheek.

"Too sweet, if you ask me," I mumble under my breath.

"Huh?" Sami asks, looking at me inquisitively.

I shake my head. "Nothing."

Sami's gaze shifts from me to my brother and back again. "I think I'm going to go sit out with the boys for a bit. Give you guys a chance to talk." She rests her hand on Snow's shoulder. "I'm sure you want to hear all about your sister's appointment, see the pictures."

Snow whirls around, a wooden spoon in his hand. "You got pictures?"

"Yep."

"Is it a boy or girl?" he asks excitedly.

Sami silently excuses herself while I stand there and stare at my brother. Of course he thinks I'm going to tell him. There was a time I told him everything. But that time came to a screeching halt when I had to start hiding my love life from him.

"I don't know," I answer him honestly.

"But Sami said you would find out today."

"I'm sure she did. And I could have found out." I sit down at their dining table and cross my arms over my chest. "But I chose not to."

"Why? I thought for sure you'd want to know."

"I did want to know. I still do. But..."

He turns the stove off and moves the pan away from the hot burner. After scooping pasta into a bowl and setting it in front of me, he sits down.

"But what?"

I swirl my fork in the long butter and garlic covered

noodles. "Nothing." I shove the bite into my mouth. "Mmm."

"No, it's not nothing. What were you going to say?"

I take three more bites before even entertaining the thought of answering him. It's kind of fun to watch him squirm.

"Zeke, why bother? It's not like you listen to me. It's pointless to have this discussion."

"Try me."

I take a deep breath and think back to my baby's heartbeat. "It felt wrong, okay? Finding that out without Magic."

He falls back against his chair. "Oh."

"Oh? That's all you've got to say? Oh?" I push my plate across the table, no longer hungry. "Zeke, I get it that you're trying to protect me, but Magic isn't who I need protecting from." I stand and begin to pace. "And I also get club rules and bylaws. I know you had to punish him for lying. But don't you get it? He's not the only one you're hurting here." I run my hand through my hair. "Shit. I can't stop torturing myself wondering how he feels."

Snow sits there quietly for a moment before leaning forward and bracing his arms on the table. "Trust me, he loves you."

"That's just it. How am I supposed to trust that? Before, he had no problem breaking the rules to see me, but now?" I shake my head. "He's just folded like a cheap deck of cards."

"Or he loves you so much, he's doing what he's told so when the six months is up, nothing will stand between the two of you."

I stop and face him and am shocked to see doubt in his eyes. The problem is, I don't know if it's that he's doubting what he said or doubting the punishment he ordered.

Praying it's the punishment, I take a risk and ask him for a favor.

"Zeke, I need to see Magic." I rush to continue so he doesn't have a chance to cut me off. "It doesn't have to be long, and you can be there." I lift the envelopes off the table. "But I need to show him these. Please? I want him to see his baby, I want to find out the gender. Please, Zeke, ask him to come over for a few minutes."

He takes a deep breath and nods. "Ok."

"Why can't you think of anyone else but—"

"Laney, I said okay." He gets his cell phone and types out a quick text. "He'll be here in a minute."

I rush toward my brother and throw myself at him. "Thank you." My feet dangle as he holds me in a hug, and I kiss him on the cheek. "Thank you, thank you, thank you."

CHAPTER 15
MAGIC

Snow: My house NOW!

I shove my cell back into my pocket and break out into a run. When Snow says to get somewhere now, he means get there five minutes ago. I don't know exactly what's going on, but it can't be anything good with that sort of demand.

When I round the corner of the road that winds through the Satan's Legacy MC compound, his house comes into view. Everything looks normal, with Sami and the boys outside playing with a frisbee. I don't bother slowing down to talk to them as I race across the yard and barrel through the front door.

Skidding to a stop, I take in the scene before me. Snow has Laney lifted off the floor in a big hug and she's kissing his cheek with excitement.

My heart skips a beat as I think about why he would want me here. Everything seems fine. Better than fine actually. Maybe he's going to lift my sentence and Laney's lips will be on me next. Or maybe she found out she's not really pregnant and she's happy because she no longer has to deal with the bullshit that comes along with being with me.

Stop it! Stop fabricating scenarios. Just ask what's going on.

I clear my throat and they separate quickly. My eyes latch onto Laney, the joy on her face, the way her clothes hug her body, the way she's changing as the pregnancy progresses. Her stomach has a slight bump, and all I want to do is go to her and kiss it.

I dart my eyes to Snow, knowing I'm treading on thin ice.

"Uh, Prez, you wanted to see me?"

"You two have ten minutes. And I'll be here the whole time, so no funny business."

Snow walks toward the hallway and disappears around the corner. So much for being here the whole time.

And you're complaining? You've got Laney all to yourself for the first time in how long?

Nerves race up my spine as I focus my attention on her. I never had this problem before. I was always comfortable around Laney. But things are different now. The question is, are they too different?

"Hi," she says, lowering her eyes to the floor.

"Hey." I take a few steps in her direction but stop myself from getting too close. "Not that I'm complaining, but why am I here?"

"I, um..." She locks eyes with me. "I asked Snow if I could see you."

"Oh."

"I went to the doctor today." She thrusts an envelope at me. "Thought you'd want to see this."

Rather than take it from her, I stare at it like it's grown tentacles. What's in there? What if her cancer is back? What if it's a dear John letter? Fuck, what if it's a letter from Marlene?

"It's an ultrasound of the baby," she finally says when I still haven't taken the envelope.

I grab it from her, and tear open the flap. My eyes land on the black and white image, and air whooshes from my lungs.

"Oh, wow," I mumble.

Laney moves to stand next to me and begins pointing at the picture. "Those are the legs, and there are the arms. He's perfect."

I whip my head to look at her. "He?"

She shrugs. "Actually, I don't know. It didn't feel right to find out without you." She lifts the other envelope she's holding. "But the answer is in here, if you want to know."

"Do you want to know?"

She smiles. "Yes."

"Me too."

Laney rips into the envelope, but before she can pull out the piece of paper, I rest my hand on hers to stop her.

"Wait."

Confusion fills her eyes. "What is it?"

"Before we look at this, I need to know something."

"Okay."

"When the six months is up, what then? Because I don't think I can—"

"I knew it," she says, her expression hardening. "You don't want to be with me anymore. I knew there was a reason you weren't coming around."

"Yeah, I was ordered not to," I remind her, taking a step back. "Do you have any idea how much this fucking sucks? I hate not being with you." Her face begins to soften. "But I refuse to do anything that could push Snow over the edge.

If I can get through these six months, we can be together. We can be a family. That's all I'm trying to do. Get through this as best I can."

"So you still want to be with me?"

"Is that a serious question?" When she nods, my shoulders slump. "Jesus, Laney, I love you. Nothing will ever change that. *Nothing*. I'll go away if you want me to, but it won't be quietly." I reach out and cup her cheek. "Tell me you still love me too."

"Of course I do." She grabs my hand and moves it to her chest. Her heart feels like it's going to thump through her skin. "I will always love you, Magic. You're the father of my child. But I don't want you to be with me out of obligation. And I certainly don't want to come between you and Satan's Legacy. That's all I was trying to do... protect you."

I chuckle. "Really? You're going to protect me?" I shake my head. "No, Laney. I protect what's mine, and that is you."

"Careful, you're starting to sound like my brother."

"Yeah, well, that's not my intention. I know you can take care of yourself. I don't doubt your abilities one bit. But if you think I'm going to step aside and take in your life like I'm watching a movie, you're nuts."

"I don't expect you to stand by the wayside, Magic. I just..." She takes a deep breath. "I want to be equals. I want us to make decisions together, be partners."

"You know that's not always possible."

"Yes, I do. I will stay in my lane where the club is concerned, but that doesn't mean I don't have opinions or won't worry. I know what's expected of me. But I never have been or will be the type to sit on the sidelines and be kept in the dark completely. I can live without details of what you do, what the club does, unless it has to do with me."

"I think I can manage that."

"Good."

"One minute left." We both look toward the hallway and see Snow standing there. "I suggest you get to that envelope."

Laney rolls her eyes, but her lips lift into a grin. "Well, do you want to know?"

I nod.

She pulls out the piece of paper, and her eyes light up and shine with a well of tears. She flips the paper around so I can see, and I can feel my eyes doing the same thing.

"Holy shit," I say under my breath. "We're having a girl."

CHAPTER 16
LANEY

A girl.

We're having a girl.

A girl? What the hell am I supposed to do with a girl?

Boys, I know. I can do boys. They're easy. But a girl? I shudder at the thought of puberty.

"Congrats you two," Snow says as he walks back into the kitchen. "Think about it Laney... there's gonna be a mini you running around before you know it."

I am thinking about it, asshole. I'm so screwed.

Magic pulls me toward him and settles his arms around my waist. He presses a kiss in my hair and then leans close to my ear.

"I can't wait to have a little you running around," he whispers. "I hope she looks just like her mommy."

"Oh, Laney. Right about now, I imagine you're thinking about all the times you snuck out of the house, all the times you got into trouble when you were younger," Snow taunts. He slaps a hand on Magic's back, jolting both of us in the process. "Good luck, brother. If your daughter is anything like my sister, you're gonna need it."

"Shut up, Zeke," I snap, stepping away from Magic. "I'm thinking no such thing."

"Okay. Next, you're going to try and tell me that grass is red." He throws his head back and laughs. "Karma... what a bitch."

"At least we know that our daughter won't suffer from a lack of confidence," Magic says, glaring at Snow. "If she's anything like her uncle, that is."

"Fine, fine. I'll stop." Snow shakes Magic's hand. "Really, brother, I'm happy for you." He pulls me closer to him. "Both of you. This is great."

"Thanks."

Snow steps in between us, forcing us apart. "Now, I'm done being nice. Your ten minutes are up."

"Right."

Magic turns to walk out of the house, but Snow stops him.

"Before you go, I've got something I want to ask Laney, and I think you should be here for it."

Magic slowly turns back around and arches a brow. "Ooookay."

"Laney, earlier you said you needed protection from someone."

I think back to our conversation before Magic arrived and shake my head. "No, I didn't."

"Yeah, you did," he insists. "You said, and I quote, 'I get it that you're trying to protect me, but Magic isn't who I need protecting from'."

"Not exactly the same thing." I laugh nervously because I know I'm splitting hairs.

"Close enough. Who were you talking about?"

"Laney," Magic says, stepping closer. "What happened?"

I huff out a breath, annoyed at my own carelessness. "Nothing. I just thought I saw someone when I left the doctor's office, but I was mistaken."

Snow and Magic exchange a look, one that tells me they're being as deceptive as I am.

"Who'd you see?" Snow asks.

"It's crazy really." I fold my hands in front of me. "I mean, he's dead, so I couldn't have seen him."

"Cedric?" Magic asks, more concerned than I've ever heard him.

"Well, yeah, but it couldn't have been him. He's..." I dart my eyes between the two of them and take in the fact that they aren't immediately reassuring me. "He *is* dead, right?"

"Yes." Magic averts his gaze. "He should be."

Fear squeezes my chest, making it hard to breathe. "What do you mean 'he should be'? You killed him, Magic. Three years ago. That's what you said. You said you killed him."

He glances at Snow, who gives a tight nod, and then Magic closes the distance between us. He lifts my hands and rubs circles over them with his thumbs.

"Laney, I did. I burnt his house down with him tied to a chair inside. There's no way he should've survived."

"But? I sense a big 'but' coming."

Snow walks to a drawer and opens it to pull out a folded-up paper. He hands it to me.

"This came the other day. It's from Marlene."

I take the letter and scan it before lifting my eyes back up to look at Magic.

"You didn't kill him? Cedric is alive?"

"We don't know. Marlene could just be trying to scare

us." His face scrunches up like his next words will pain him to say. "But yes, there's a possibility he somehow survived."

I suck in a breath, then another, and then another. My head spins and a buzzing fills my ears.

Magic rubs his hands up and down my arms. "Laney, breathe. I need you to breathe for me."

"This can't..." Another breath. "This can't be happening."

"We don't know that it is," Snow chimes in. "We're digging as deep as we can to figure out what's going on."

I pull away from them and start toward the door. "I can't do this right now. I gotta go." I walk out of the house and race down the porch steps. "Shiloh, time to go home." I grab his hand after he throws the frisbee and practically drag him behind me.

"Laney, wait," Sami calls. "Are you okay?"

"Fine," I toss over my shoulder.

"Mom, what's wrong?"

I look at my son, take in the fear in his eyes. I force myself to stop walking and kneel down so I'm at eye level.

"Nothing's wrong, Shi. I'm just not feeling well so it's time to go home."

"Why can't I stay?"

I look past him and see Magic and Snow standing on the porch, Sami and Lennox in front of them. All of them look worried. I take a deep breath and stand straight.

"Sami, is it okay if Shiloh stays for a while? I can pick him up later."

As much as I don't want to be alone, what I have to work through is too much for a ten-year-old. And it's not fair for me to put him through what I don't even want to go through.

"Of course," she says. "I'll bring him home after dinner."

"That work for you?" I ask Shiloh.

He nods.

"Sounds good, Sami. Thanks." I kiss Shiloh on the forehead. "Go, have fun."

Shiloh hesitates, looking back and forth between me and his best friend. "Are you sure you're okay, Mom?"

"Absolutely," I lie. "I'll see ya later."

"Okay. Bye."

He takes off running back toward the house, leaving me utterly and completely alone. I hate being alone, especially when I'm scared. I put on this tough exterior, try to make others see me as stronger than I am, but the truth is, Cedric scares me. Not only can he hurt me physically, but he can take away the very thing that I live for: Shiloh.

I slowly make my way home. My brain is a pile of sludge, but my heart might as well be a Kentucky Derby winner. When I let myself inside, I make sure to lock the door. Then I text Snow and ask him to let me know when Shiloh's on his way home so I can let him in.

I glance around at the living room. It could use a good dusting, but I don't have it in me to care. Instead, I go to my bedroom, lay on the bed, and pull the covers up over my head.

Maybe I can sleep away my worst nightmare.

"I'll find you, Laney. You and Shiloh can't hide forever."

I place a hand over Shiloh's mouth and keep my stare pinned to the sliver of light coming under the closet door. I don't know how Cedric got onto the compound, but at this point, it doesn't matter. I can dwell on that later.

"She's gotta be here somewhere."

Marlene's voice is scratchy, as if she's been chain smoking for years. A shadow mars the stream of light, and I know it won't be long before the closet door is thrown open. Then what?

I'm startled awake by a noise, and I scoot into a sitting position, straining my ears to see if I hear it again.

There! A creaking noise. Footsteps. Was my nightmare some kind of warning?

I reach over and slowly open the drawer on my nightstand. I punch in the code to the small safe I keep inside, and when it opens, I lift my 9mm, the suppressor already screwed on. When I bought the two, Shiloh was much younger, and if I ever found myself in a position to use the gun, I wanted to be able to do so without my son knowing.

Armed, I climb out of bed and tiptoe to the door. I press my ear to the wood while pointing the 9mm toward the ground. My arms are loose, but I'm ready for whatever awaits me on the other side.

You can do this, Laney. You're no stranger to guns. Your brother and Magic made sure of that.

Turning the knob, I open the door. I'm grateful when it doesn't squeak, and then I remember that Magic had put WD-40 on it not long before hell came knocking. I lean around the frame and see a shadow moving. Whoever it is must be in the kitchen, because I can't see them.

I creep down the hall, my arms extended, my finger on the trigger. When I reach the living room, I see a figure, standing in the dark near the kitchen island, but facing the cabinets. My hands begin to tremble. I've never shot a person before. Pop cans, coffee cans, targets... sure. But not people.

The man reaches into his pocket, and I pull the trigger. The sound of shattering glass reaches my ears the same time the man's exclamation does.

"Holy shit!"

Magic?

I flip the switch next to me and flood the room in light. Magic is standing there, his eyes wide and his hands up like a caught cat-burglar.

"What the fuck are you doing here?" I demand, lowering my gun and stomping toward him. "I almost shot you!"

"I'm very aware," he says and turns his head to look at what remains of the beer bottle he's holding.

"What are you doing here?" I ask again.

"I came to check on you." He tosses the broken bottle into the trash and leans against the counter. "I was worried after the way you left. And then Snow couldn't get a hold of you to bring Shiloh home, so I—"

"Shit." My eyes dart to the clock on the microwave. It's the middle of the fucking night. I rub a hand over my forehead. "I can't believe I slept so long."

"And so hard. When I first got here, I looked in the bedroom and saw you sleeping, so I thought I'd come out here and drink the rest of my beer before I woke you up." He shrugs. "Guess I wasn't as quiet as I thought."

"No, you weren't," I snap. "I thought you were... never mind."

"Cedric. You thought I was Cedric."

"He's dead."

"Most likely."

"Right." I pull a chair out and sit down, setting my 9mm in the middle of the table. "Wait a second. If my brother couldn't get a hold of me, how come he didn't come check on me?" If there really is a chance that Cedric is alive, it makes no sense that Snow would choose now to stop protecting me.

"He did. Said you were sleeping," Magic informs me.

How many people paraded through my house while I slept?

"But you were still worried?"

Magic walks around the table and turns the entire chair, with me in it, around to face him. He grabs my hands and pulls me to stand.

"I always worry about you, Laney." He threads his hands in my hair and leans in to kiss me. When he breaks the contact, he says, "Always."

It's been so long since he's touched me, other than the hug earlier at Snow's house. And that doesn't begin to compare to what I experience now. I miss Magic's touch. I miss his mouth, his body... him.

Then a thought hits me, icing over my fast-melting insides. I push away from him.

"So, you do still know how to sneak in?"

Magic's face hardens, and his eyes narrow. "Don't, Laney."

"Don't what? Call 'em like I see 'em?"

"No, don't make accusations that you know aren't true. You know why I stayed away. But tonight..." He heaves a sigh. "I just couldn't. Not with how upset you were when you stormed out of Snow's earlier."

"And if you get caught?"

Magic grins. "I won't. Your brother, in his infinite wisdom, put two prospects on the house. Told them to watch the doors." He rolls his eyes. "Oh, they're guarding the doors alright. Both pacing back and forth like sentries at the front and back... of the wrong goddamned house."

My hand flies to my mouth to stifle the laugh barreling up my chest. "Oh, no."

"Oh yes. I imagine they won't be around much longer." He cracks his knuckles. "I'm kinda hoping Snow leaves their punishment to me. I could use a little me time."

"I'm sure you could."

Magic takes a deep breath and reaches out for me. I hesitate for only a moment before stepping into his arms. Relaxing into him, I feel safe, loved. And my anger and annoyance are gone.

"Can you believe we're having a girl?" he asks, holding me tight.

"No."

"Hmm, I can. I hope she's a spitfire like you."

I lift my head and look him in the eyes. "Really? Because that thought scares the hell out of me."

"Oh yeah," he says. "She'll be smart, beautiful, independent, strong beyond words... she'll be perfect." Magic screws up his face. "I just hope she doesn't get my penchant for violence. That could be bad." He flattens his palm over my stomach. "Maybe we should start playing classical music for her now, even out the odds a bit."

"Classic rock, maybe."

"That too."

I lift my arms and link my hands behind his neck. "Ya know, we didn't really get to enjoy the news this afternoon."

"No, we didn't."

"Maybe we should take advantage of the time we have now. Because it's all we'll have for a few more months, unless you keep sneaking in."

"This is not going to be a repeat performance. I'd love to

come back every night, but if I get caught again, who knows what will happen?"

I jump up and Magic catches me easily. He clasps his hands under my ass and starts walking toward my bedroom.

"We better make it count," I whisper just before touching the tip of my tongue to his bottom lip.

"Yeah, we probably should."

Magic swirls his tongue around mine and then nibbles on my lips. When we reach the bed, he gently lays me down and crawls over me.

"Are you ready?" he asks between kisses. "Because this needs to last us a few months."

I moan into his mouth, giving him the only answer I'm capable of.

And Magic delivers. We make memories that could last a lifetime… if I weren't such a greedy woman.

CHAPTER 17
MAGIC

"Aw, c'mon honey."

Lorna rakes her fingernails over my chest, the long red tips feeling like claws trying to rip me apart. I grab her hands and shove them away.

"Not interested."

"Sure ya are," she says, batting her eyes like that will help.

"Nope."

She reaches out to touch me again, but I grip her wrists and squeeze.

"I told you, not interested. Walk away."

Lorna pouts, but it doesn't last long when Spark slides up behind her and wraps his arms around her to squeeze her tits.

"Turn that frown upside down, darlin'. Spark's here to make it all better."

As if I don't exist, Lorna focuses her attention on Spark, and they work their way into the crowd of other club whores and brothers dancing.

I've been dodging girls left and right tonight. There's no

124

need to put on a show anymore and pretend to enjoy their interest. Everyone knows about Laney and me, so why bother?

I lift a hand to Little Man, signaling for another drink. It takes him a full minute to set the whiskey in front of me, which is sixty seconds too long. I lift the glass to my lips but am interrupted before I can take a drink.

"Hey, sugar."

I recognize the voice and internally cringe. I down the entire glass of Jack Daniels and slam it on the bar before turning to face the woman.

"Not happening, Minnie."

She pokes her bottom lip out. "Oh, you poor thing. I heard about..." She leans in and cups a hand around her mouth to whisper, "Laney."

I stiffen, pissed off that the gossip has reached the whores. Their job is to mingle and keep the guys happy, not interfere in business that doesn't concern them.

"Don't give a shit what you heard." I glare at her. "Go find another cock to play with."

"I suggest you check your tone."

I look to my other side and see Snow standing there. He doesn't look happy, and it doesn't take a genius to figure out why. I stifle a groan.

"Minnie, will you excuse us a minute?" Snow smiles at her, but the dismissal is clear.

She walks away and settles into a group of unsuspecting hang arounds. They look young, maybe early twenties, and I suspect they're nowhere near ready for Minnie's introduction into the fine art of seduction.

"If I hear you talk to a woman that way again, there will be—"

"Hell to pay," I finish for him. "Yeah, I know."

"Don't get smart," he barks. "Aren't you in enough trouble already?"

"Go easy on him, Prez," Duck says with a chuckle as he joins us at the bar. "No doubt the guy hasn't been laid since, well, since you banned him from seeing Laney. You try and go this long without pussy and see how pleasant you are."

"Too far, Duck," Snow snaps. "Besides, it's his own damn fault, and I don't give a flying fuck how long it's been since he's gotten any. We don't treat women like mosquitos to be flicked away."

"He knows that," Toga says as he steps up next to Duck. "And he's only turned down, what, five chicks tonight? Could be worse. He could've left with the first one and pissed Laney off."

"I'd worry he wouldn't know what to do with someone else." Duck laughs. "He's a bit out of practice. Might give Satan's Legacy a bad name. With the ladies, that is."

"Oh my God, what a horror show that would be," Dip quips as he joins the group. "Parties without the ladies. No thank you."

"Motherfucker," I shout. "I'm standing right here, ya know?"

"Oh, I didn't see you there," Toga jokes and glances at the others. "Did any of you see him there?"

"Shut up." I lean over the bar and grab the bottle of Jack Daniels Little Man set down after pouring my last drink. I take a pull to calm myself, but it doesn't do anything. "Can't a man drink in peace?"

"Sure, when he remembers his manners." Snow smacks me on the back, a little too hard. "What is wrong with you tonight?"

Oh, I don't know. It's been a week since I was with Laney. It's going to be another few months, and I don't want to be with anyone else in the meantime. Pick your poison.

"Nothin'."

"Well, whatever it is, get it in check."

"Fine."

We stand there, the five of us drinking our booze and watching the party. My eyes drift to the door, seeking out the only person who could turn this night around. So what if I can't touch her? Seeing Laney is still a far cry better than enduring the false charms of any other woman on the planet.

"She's at home with Shiloh."

I glance at Snow out of the corner of my eye. It makes sense that she's home. She hasn't been to many club parties since she found out she's pregnant. A smile plays on my lips at the thought of her curled up on the couch, a throw blanket on her lap, and Shiloh hugged up against her while they watch a movie.

"I figured."

"Well stop figuring," Snow barks. "It's getting on my nerves."

"Sure thing, Prez," I say sarcastically. "I'll just forget all about her and my baby."

"Magic, this isn't a path you want——"

"So, Prez," Dip interrupts. "Before this turns into a brawl, I've got some info." He lifts his cell phone and shakes it. "Heard back from several of my contacts just before I came in tonight."

My body stiffens. This is it. Either confirmation that I'm damn good at my job, or that I'm incompetent as hell and Cedric is alive. At this point, I'm not entirely sure which I'd prefer. The thought of getting another crack at the man, really bloodying him up, is enticing as hell.

"And?" Snow prods when Dip doesn't go on.

"Well," Dip glances at me and the look in his eyes is one of pity. "Cedric is alive."

The beer bottle Snow was holding shatters behind the bar, sending spider-web cracks spreading in the mirror like wildfire. His fists clench at his sides and he focuses on me.

"Magic, this is on you."

No shit.

"There's more," Dip states.

I reach down and grab the knife in my boot. Running my fingers over the blade, I contemplate all the ways I'm going to make Cedric pay for not dying.

"Where is he?" I ask. My voice is calm but I'm the furthest thing from it.

"Apparently, brother and sister are bouncing from campground to campground. From what my sources tell me, they never stay in one place too long. Some say they're using assumed names, while others aren't sure. He might have scars from the fire, he might not."

"In other words, we know nothing other than he breathes the same air we do?"

"I'm sorry, Magic. I wish I had more solid intel." Dip shoves his phone in his pocket. "I'll keep digging. One guy did give me the name of the last campground they were allegedly at, but I haven't had a chance to confirm anything."

"Okay." Snow claps him on the back. "Gather up the others and bring them to the meeting room. Seems like we've got some work to do."

"There's no time for church," I protest and move my knife back and forth so the minimal light in the main room glints off the blade. "We need to go now, track them down and get rid of them."

"And we will do both of those things," Snow agrees. "After church."

"I don't fucking think so."

I turn to walk away, but Snow grabs the back of my cut and Dip blocks my path.

"It's an order, Magic, not a request," Snow growls. "Get in the meeting room. Now."

I jerk out of his hold but remain in place. I want to argue, to tell him to fuck off, but I can't. Not now, not while I'm already in trouble. I glance at my knife and heave a sigh before putting it back in its sheath.

"This is a waste of time, and you know it."

"No, I don't know it." Snow steps around to my front. "But I do know it's how we operate. Meeting. Room. Now."

Unbelievable. As protective of Laney and Shiloh as Snow is, he's really dropping the ball with this. We could find Cedric and Marlene tonight and eliminate the problem. But, oh no, we have to follow the rules.

Not following the rules got you in trouble once. Don't push it.

I stomp toward the room and sit in my usual chair. It takes ten more minutes for the others to file in, all of whom are in varied states of drunkenness.

This should be real productive.

CHAPTER 18

LANEY

I step out onto the sidewalk in front of the building that houses my doctor's office. The air is cold, but the sun is shining. I lift my eyes to the sky and smile as a few snowflakes land on my face. It's the first snow of the year and no major accumulation is expected, but it's still pretty.

Looking both ways, I cross the street to where I parked Snow's truck. I need new tires on my car and haven't gotten around to it yet, so Snow let me borrow his vehicle. While it's good in the snow, the heat leaves something to be desired. It's on its last leg.

I'm hyper aware of my surroundings, now that I know for sure that it was Cedric I saw at my last appointment. Thinking back to the moment Snow told me he was still alive, my mind reels. Normally, I wouldn't be alone, but the prospect Snow sent with me got a call and took off. He was kind enough to leave a note with the receptionist and the truck so I wouldn't be stranded.

So kind of him... stupid fucker.

I hope the emergency was worth it because there's gonna be hell to pay when Snow finds out.

After I settle into the driver's seat, I lock the doors. I start the engine and then rub my hands in front of the vents in an attempt to warm them with what little heat is being expelled. It takes a few minutes, but I don't dawdle too long before pulling away from the curb and heading home.

The farther I get away from the city, the faster snow is coming down and sticking to the roads. The higher elevations always seem to get it the worst. When I make the last turn that leads me into no man's land, I lean forward to better see where I'm going. Unless the club does it, these roads don't get plowed or salted much. No doubt, no one has had the time to do either.

A car turns behind me, but I don't think anything of it and continue down the road, squinting out the windshield to see through the storm. I gasp as my body jerks when the truck rocks from a hit to the rear.

"What the hell?" I glance in my mirror in time to see them slow down. I can't make out who's in the vehicle, but it appears to only be one person.

I press on the brake to slow down and ease to the side so they can pass, although I don't know why they would. Unless it's someone that has business with Satan's Legacy. Not my problem. They'll be stopped at the gate and whoever is on duty can deal with them.

My eyes widen when instead of going around me, they ram the back of the truck again. Lurching forward, I feel the moment the truck's front tire slips off the side of the road, and panic sets in.

When the SUV backs up and then lurches forward again, I reach for my purse to get my cell phone. This time, they hit the back side of the truck bed and it skids sideways, sending my purse and its contents to the floorboard.

I lean over to try and reach it, but the seat belt holds me back.

"Son of a bitch," I mutter as I fumble to unbuckle myself.

My head bounces off the steering wheel as I'm hit again, and then again. Blood trickles out of the fresh cut, and I reach up to feel my hair becoming wet and sticky.

I feel the baby kick and breathe a sigh of relief that she seems to be okay. Whoever the fucker is behind me is going to suffer, but kill my baby and they'll have to answer to more than the club. Hell hath no fury like a woman...

Free from my constraints, I reach for my purse again. I haul it back to the seat and dig for my cell. Just as my hand wraps around it, the truck is hit again, only this time, it goes completely off the road and rolls, tossing me about like a rag doll. When it comes to a stop, the truck is upside down, and I'm lying on the cold metal of the roof.

I press my hand against my stomach, trying to feel the baby move again, but I can't feel a damn thing past the pain. Tears stream down my face, clouding my vision as they mix with blood. I feel around for my phone, having lost my grip in the chaos of rolling.

My fingertips barely touch it, so I scoot myself toward the passenger side. Once I've got a hold on it, I bring the cell to my face and try to see the buttons.

Unable to make anything out, I slowly run my hands over the screen and punch in a number I hope is right.

"Laney, you shouldn't be calling me," Magic says by way of greeting. "What if—"

"Help," I choke out. "Ma-Magic, I need y-you."

Magic

HELP. I need you.

Laney went silent after those words. I tried to get her to answer me, say something, but she didn't... or couldn't.

I hit the speed dial for Snow, and he answers on the third ring.

"I need you to track Laney's phone," I bark.

"Why?" he asks suspiciously. "You don't need—"

"Snow, just do it! I know you monitor her location."

I fly down the road in my truck, grateful I chose to drive it and not my Harley. The snow is really coming down.

"What is going on?" he demands.

"Where is she?"

There's a moment of silence before Snow says, "She's on her way home from the doctor. On the last road before turning into the compound."

"Hang on, Laney," I mumble.

"Magic, what the fuck is going on?"

"I don't know. She called and..." My words trail off as I see the tires of a vehicle up in the air off the side of the road. "Holy shit."

"Get Carnie to your house. I gotta go."

I disconnect the call and throw the phone onto the seat as I hop out of my truck. It rings almost immediately, and I know it's Snow. He's no doubt freaking out, wanting more information, wanting to get in his truck and come to the rescue.

I stumble down the hill and am grateful to see that it's Snow's truck on its roof. Now he has no choice but to do as I said. Even he's not stupid enough to hop on his Harley and race here.

"Laney!" I call out to her.

I see her laying inside, but she's not moving. I pull on the door handle, and it doesn't budge. Bracing my boot on the side of the truck, I yank as hard as I can. It takes some muscle, but I manage to get it open.

"Laney." Blood coats her hair at her temple. I feel for a wound and find a small gash, one that shouldn't require more than stitches. Moving my hands, I settle them under her. "Laney, answer me."

"Ma-Magic."

"Yeah, Sweet Cheeks, I'm here. Can you move?"

"I th-think so."

"Okay, I'm going to try and pull you out as gently as I can. If it's too much, just yell at me."

Laney nods, a groan escaping her as she does.

Gently, I move her inch by inch until she clears the open door. I lift her in my arms and her head settles onto my shoulder. I start up the hill toward my truck.

"I'm gonna get you home. Carnie should already be there."

"Okay." She lifts her eyes to mine and they're shiny. "What about the baby? I haven't felt her move since..." Her bottom lip quivers, and she averts her gaze.

I settle her into the passenger seat and splay my palm over her stomach. I don't feel anything at first, and I begin to panic.

"I'm sure she's..." A flutter against my hand startles me. "Ah, there she is."

"You felt her?" Her eyes widen. "Oh wait, there she is. Thank God."

Laney flops her head back against the seat and closes

her eyes. "Green SUV, earlier model Jeep maybe." She shrugs. "I don't know."

The hair on the back of my neck stands up. "This wasn't an accident?"

"No."

Cedric.

I close her door and rush to the driver's side. I never shut the truck off, so I put it in gear and haul ass, as safely as possible, to the compound. Spark is at the gate, and Snow must have tipped him off because he has it open before I even reach it.

"Thanks, brother," I yell out the window, and he lifts his hand in response.

I skid to a stop in front of Snow's house, and he races down the steps to yank open the passenger door.

"Laney," he says on an exhale, looking over her. "What the hell happened?"

"Got run off..."

I miss the rest of her words as I get out and race around to her door. Without even thinking, I push Snow out of the way and lift Laney into my arms.

"Carnie inside?" I ask as I make my way toward the porch.

"Of course he is," Snow snaps, falling into step beside me. "Did you see who did this?"

"Nope, gone by the time I got there. I'm sure there are tracks, but I was more concerned about your sister."

If looks could kill, Laney would be on the floor right now with the glare Snow directs at me.

"Would you two cut the shit," Carnie snaps when we reach the spare bedroom. "Put her down here." He points to the bed.

"Hey, Carn," Laney says as I lay her down.

Snow and I step back to let Carnie work.

"Hiya, honey." Carnie starts at Laney's head, inspecting the gash that I felt. "Ya know, if you wanted to see me, all ya had to do was call. I'd have come for a visit."

"Yeah, but I wanted to be sure," Laney jokes, although there's no humor in her tone. "So, what's the damage?"

"Can you tell me what happened?"

"I was on my way home from my appointment and got run off the road." She winces when he presses around the gash. "Actually, it was more like an ambush."

"What do you mean?" Snow snaps.

Laney lifts her eyes to her brother, and Carnie rests his hand on her shoulder. "Focus on me, honey." He looks back at Snow and me. "These two were just leaving."

"You don't give the orders around here," Snow barks.

Carnie stands and walks toward us, pressing his hands against our chests and backing us toward the door.

"Do you want me to be so distracted that I miss something?" Carnie tips his head. "Not to mention, scaring the shit out of Laney more than she already is? Let me do my job."

"We need information," I tell Carnie, taking Snow's side on this.

"And I'll get it." Carnie looks over his shoulder at Laney, who's staring at the three of us intently. "While I do that, I suggest you get someone to the scene to see if anything there is of significance."

"You've got thirty minutes," Snow says behind clenched teeth.

"I've got as long as it takes."

Snow looks over Carnie's shoulder at his sister. "Laney, I'll be right outside if you need me, okay?"

"I know." She shifts her gaze to me. "And you?"

"Not going anywhere, Sweet Cheeks."

I dart a look at Snow, daring him to enforce my punishment. I'm grateful, but shocked, when he doesn't.

CHAPTER 19

MAGIC

"Where's our VP, Prez?"

Snow rolls his eyes at Dip, who's leaning back in his chair so far, it's about to tip over.

"I'm perfectly capable of running a session without Duck. And he's at the shelter for his shift tonight."

Dip lifts his hands in front of him. "Just giving you a hard time, brother."

"Which is why you're not on the floor in a puddle of blood."

"Noted."

Snow shifts his eyes to the rest of us. "Anyone else wanna try their comedy routine?"

When everyone remains quiet, Snow pulls his chair out and sits down.

"As you all know, Laney was targeted this afternoon." He holds his hand up to silence those already calling out questions. "She's fine. Banged up and shaken, but fine. My truck on the other hand..."

"Ah, we'll get the dents out and sand down the scratches," Spark says. "Fresh paint job and it'll be good as new."

"Appreciate it," Snow says and sighs. "Anyway, my truck is really the least of my concerns." He looks at Carnie. "Fill 'em in on Laney so we can move on."

"Not much to say," Carnie begins. "I stitched up a gash on her temple. She wasn't happy about that because she couldn't have any of the prescription pain meds I keep on hand because of the pregnancy. I did give her Tylenol, for all the good it did. Normally I'd resort to liquor, but sa—"

"Carnie!" Snow slams his fist on the table. "We don't need the scenic route."

"Right." Carnie shifts in his seat. "Stitched the gash up, shouldn't leave too big of a scar. Checked the baby... heartbeat was strong, she was kicking up a storm. I had Fallon and Sami take her back to the doctor to be sure. All was good. She's got a lot of bruises, but after a day or two of rest, Laney will be fine."

"Any questions?" Snow gives the brothers a chance to speak up, but no one does. He shifts. "Toga, what did you find at the scene?"

"It's clear by the tire tracks that Laney didn't stand a chance. And she was right." He slides a photo across the table. "Older model Jeep. Cherokee to be exact. Not sure if it's a vehicle that hasn't been driven a lot or if they replaced the tires, but they're what the SUV goes off the showroom floor with."

"Good. Brady, were you able to track the Jeep down?"

"I've narrowed it down to four people who drive an older style dark green Jeep Cherokee. Three of them we can rule out. Their phones put them in the city at the time of the accident."

"And the fourth?" I ask, leaning forward.

"That one's a little tricky. The SUV is registered to a..."

He looks down at the paper in front of him. "... Linda Tate. But here's the thing, Linda Tate is—"

"Dead," Snow finishes for him.

"Yeah, how'd you know?"

"Because Linda Tate is Marlene and Cedric's mother. Tate is her maiden name."

"So the Jeep belongs to Marlene?"

"I assume so since it's registered in a woman's name."

"What's the address where the Jeep is registered?" Snow asks Brady.

"The address is in Littleton." He taps the paper. "It's all here."

"Dip," Snow turns to him. "Did any of your contacts say anything about Littleton?"

"Not a word. But that doesn't mean anything."

"Were you ever able to confirm any of the leads about them being in a campground?"

"Only what I've already told you," Dip says. "I confirmed one place they were at for a week, but that was a year ago. Nothing since."

"Makes sense," Brady says. "I took it a step further and dug into the purchase of the house in Littleton. It was bought, with cash, about a year ago."

I rise from my chair and lean my palms on the table. "I say we take them out tonight."

"I'm inclined to agree," Snow says. "But..."

"But what?" I throw my hands up in the air. "They went after your sister! What more do you need?"

"Nothing. But Cedric and Marlene aren't stupid. They'll expect something tonight." He shakes his head. "No, I say we wait a few days, make them think we haven't figured anything out. They'll let their guard down. We go in tonight and we all know what we'll find. Nothing."

"I hate to say it, Magic, but I agree."

I whirl on Toga. "Are you fucking serious? We go in loaded and they don't stand a chance. We have to go tonight."

"We go in loaded and they see us. Think, brother." Toga stands as well. "If it were you, would you go home and wait for us to show up? Or would you cover your tracks and lay low for a while?"

"What kinda question is that?"

"Exactly the kind you need to think about," Snow answers for him. "This isn't the time to play fast and loose."

"I'm not play—"

"Yes, you are!" Snow shouts. "You're too blinded by the fact that it's Laney that you're not thinking straight."

"And you are?" I counter. "Because I don't know how you possibly could be."

"No, I'm not," he concedes. "Which is why I'm playing it safe. We fuck up and Laney could pay the price. Not to mention your child."

My stomach drops. Losing Laney would destroy me but losing her and the baby would send me into a dark pit of self-torture that I'd likely never be able to stop.

"That's low, Prez," I say on a sigh.

"But apparently it was necessary."

"Fine. I'll do whatever the club wants. But don't make me wait too long because I've got an itch that only the deaths of those two will scratch."

"It won't be long," Snow assures me. He turns to face the group. "All in favor in a one week hold on our attack, raise your hand."

All hands go up.

"Good. We'll meet again before we ride."

"That it, Prez?" I ask.

"No. Magic, I want you to go to the shelter, fill Duck in."

"Why can't you just call him?"

"Because I want you to go. It'll keep you busy and my night free to spend time with my wife and not worry about you."

I flip him off and turn to walk out of the room. The sound of his laughter, mixed with the others, fades away as I walk down the hallway. When I hit the exit, I shove it open and enjoy the thud it makes when it hits the concrete wall.

My truck is parked in front of the clubhouse, but I ignore it and walk to my place. The only thing that is going to calm me down, besides a visit to Laney, is a ride on my Harley. Most of the snow has melted already, so as long as I'm careful until I hit the main roads, I'll be fine.

I straddle my bike and grin at the way it rumbles between my legs. Already feeling calmer, or at least more able to pretend I am, I turn the bike toward the front of the compound and take off.

When I reach the scene where Laney was ambushed, I slow down. Snow's truck has already been towed back to the compound, and the tire tracks disappeared with the snow, but the image of all of it is burned into my brain.

I grip the handlebars so tight my knuckles crack. What happened today is not something I'll ever forget... or forgive. I may be able to stuff it in the vault with all the other shit in my head, but that will only happen once the Milner's are dead.

The rest of my ride is filled with planning and plotting the perfect way to end their lives. The final combination of tortures I come up with involves a machete and a torch. I like it.

I park my Harley behind the shelter and walk around to

the front. I expect Heather or Duck to let me in, so I'm surprised when it's Connie, one of the other shelter employees, who answers.

"Magic," she greets me and steps aside. "Now why is the Satan's Legacy Enforcer showing up on the doorstep tonight? Our dues are paid."

I smile. "They are. I'm here to see Duck, fill him in on a situation."

"Does this have to do with Laney?" Connie leans forward, so close I can smell her perfume. "Duck told us about her accident."

"Did he now?"

Duck talks too fucking much.

"Yeah. Poor thing, sliding on black ice like that. I hope she and the baby are doing okay."

"They're both fine."

"Thank God for that." She grabs my forearm. "Congrats by the way... Daddy."

I chuckle, uncomfortable with where she's taking the conversation. It was one thing to have the entire club talking about us, but now Connie? A guy can only handle so much.

"Where can I find Duck?" I look past her, over the cots, which are half empty. "His Harley was out back, but I don't see him anywhere."

"He's in the office with Heather." She flaps her hand like it's nothing. "They like to think no one knows, but I know when Heather asks me to stay an extra hour on days where he's here, I know why."

"I'm sure you do."

I ignore Connie's continued gabbing and wind my way through the cots toward the office. Pressing my ear to the door, I roll my eyes when I hear Duck grunt. Stay in hotels with a guy so many times and you start to recognize the noises they make… even when you want to scrub your ears free of them.

I knock on the door, and the scrambling that comes through the door has me rocking back on my heels. Oh, this is good.

"Who is it?" Heather calls.

"Neighborhood watch program, ma'am."

"Magic, you motherfucker," Duck shouts from inside.

Seconds later, the door flies open, and Duck is standing there with his jeans barely on and his chest bare. I lean to look past him and see Heather buttoning her jeans and then straighten.

"Better not let Snow see your cut on the floor. You know how he gets about that shit."

"Stuff it." He turns to Heather, who's all put together. "Can you give us a minute?"

"Sure thing."

I move to the side as she walks past me and cringe when she tosses a look over her shoulder.

"Heard about the baby. Congrats Magic."

I kick the door shut behind me and pin Duck with my stare. "Sure are talking an awful lot."

"Still outrank you," he counters, a stupid grin on his face.

"Whatever." I run a hand through my hair and take a few deep breaths. "Snow wanted me to come down and fill you in on church."

"So, spit it out."

It takes me all of five minutes to do so, and the entire time, Duck is darting looks at the door, as if I'm boring him.

"Dude, are you even listening?"

"Yeah."

"No, you're—"

"Laney and the baby are fine. Brady got a lead on the vehicle and an address of Cedric and Marlene. The club voted to wait about a week to make our move." He crosses his arms over his chest. "Miss anything?"

"Well, no."

"Exactly. Now, if you'll excuse me, I've got a shift to work."

I slap my hand against his chest before he reaches the door. Duck lowers his head and when he lifts it again, his eyes are full of fire. I remove my hand and step to the side.

"So it's like that?" I ask.

His face softens the slightest bit. "I love her, bro. You, of all people, should understand that."

"I do."

"I'm gonna ask her to marry me."

"Aw, fuck, you knocked her up, didn't you?"

I don't see his fist, but my jaw sure feels it.

"Watch it, Magic. I'm not you," he seethes, shaking his hand out. "I prefer to do things the right way."

"Got it."

I move my jaw back and forth to make sure it's not broken. It hurts like hell, but I'll live.

Duck shoves past me, purposely bumping into my side as he does. I stumble but quickly right myself.

"Yeah, I definitely got it," I mutter and then my lips lift into a grin. "Fucker's gone and gotten himself an actual love life."

CHAPTER 20

LANEY

I run my hands over my belly and stare at my reflection in the full-length mirror. All my swelling has gone away in the last week, but little girl must want to stand out because my midsection continues to grow.

"C'mon, baby," I say, looking down. "Give mama a break."

My phone dings and a quick glance reminds me of my doctor's appointment this afternoon. Not that I could forget. I might as well take my sleeping bag and live there because I feel like I'm there more than I'm home.

"Laney!"

My brother's voice booms through the house. I push my shirt down and go out to the living room to meet him. Shiloh beats me to it.

"Uncle Zeke," he shrieks as he launches himself into Snow's arms.

"Hey, my man." Snow ruffles Shiloh's too long hair. "How's it hangin'?"

"Low and free."

Shiloh giggles but quickly puts his hands over his

mouth when I give him my best 'Mom isn't happy' look. I shift my focus to my brother.

"Giving him the sex talk wasn't enough? You had to teach him 'low and free'?"

Snow tugs on his ear. "You know about that?"

"Sorry, Uncle Zeke," Shiloh says. "It slipped out."

That's not exactly how I remember it happening, but I don't correct him.

"Look, Laney," Snow begins. "We were watching a movie, an *adult* scene came on, and the boys had questions."

"What movie?"

He averts his gaze. "I, uh, don't remember."

"It was American Pie, Uncle Zeke. I remember because the one guy put his—"

"Thanks, Shi," Snow stops him. "I remember now."

"I can't believe you were watching American Pie in front of the boys," I chastise.

"They were supposed to be watching their own movie in the bedroom. How was I supposed to know they'd sneak out and make themselves at home at the table?"

"They're ten," I remind him. "They're sneaky."

Snow hangs his head. "Yeah, that's what Sami said. If it makes you feel any better, I got an earful from her."

"Did she throw in a few day dry spell?"

"Dammit, Laney."

"Well, did she?"

"If you must know, it was a week-long dry spell."

"Then yes, I feel better."

"Good." Snow looks at Shiloh. "Okay, ya nark, go get your jacket. I should have been at the clubhouse five minutes ago."

Shiloh races to the closet and pulls his coat off the hanger before putting it on. "Ready."

"You sure it's okay if he's there?" I ask.

"Yeah, it's fine. Fallon is going to watch Lennox and him while church is in session. It won't last long."

I nod. Another question sits on the tip of my tongue, but I can't force myself to ask it.

"Laney, I know you well enough to know when you've got something on your mind. What is it?"

"Nothing."

"Bullshit."

"You say that a lot, ya know? Should watch that mouth of yours."

"I wouldn't say it if you were honest with me."

And I'd be honest if it didn't always backfire on me.

"Laney, c'mon," he pries.

I square my shoulders. If I'm going to do this, I need to stand my ground... or at least look like I am.

"Fine. I was going to ask you if you could revote on Magic's punishment, maybe end it early?"

"Not gonna happen."

I rest my hand on his arm. "Please, Zeke. I..." I lower my voice so Shiloh can't hear. "I'm scared here by myself."

"Then I'll have the prospects stay inside. Would that make you feel better?"

"Inside what house?" I counter.

"Yours. What other house would it be?"

"The one they actually stand guard at every night." I shake my head in disbelief. He really had no idea. "Those fucks you've got that are supposed to protect me... they've been guarding the house reserved for visiting chapters. Don't tell me no one told you?"

The look on his face says it all. He was told, probably by

several brothers, but too damn stubborn and cocky to think his plan was going exactly as it should. Idiot.

"Zeke, look, I need Magic here. I trust him. Shiloh trusts him." Running my hand over my protruding stomach, I lift my lips into a sad smile. "And he should be here. It's been a few months. Don't you think he's been punished long enough?"

"Laney, you know his sentence should have been death. As far as I'm concerned, he's gotten off easy."

"And you'd really kill a man simply for following his heart? You're a better man than that."

He shakes his head, his face falling. "No, Laney, I'm really not. We have rules for a reason. Besides, he's not being punished for being with you, he's being punished for lying. That's a sin that should be unforgivable, but we're all making an exception for you."

I take a step back. "Yeah, well, thanks for nothing." I walk to Shiloh and kiss him on the head. "Have fun with Lennox, Shi. I'll be home before dinner."

I walk out the door, leaving the two behind to stare after me. Climbing in the car, I glance back at the house and see Snow pulling the door shut. When they turn around, he wraps his arm around Shiloh's shoulder, and they walk down the steps. Shiloh is the only one who looks at me as they pass my car.

I slam the steering wheel with both hands once they round the corner and are out of view.

"Son of a bitch." Little girl kicks, clearly unhappy with mama's outburst. Resting my forehead against the wheel, I look down and speak to her. "Sorry, baby. Didn't mean to scare you."

Why are you caving?

The question circles in my mind, taunting me to put up

a fight for what I want, what I know is right. But it's not that simple. I tried to protect Magic and he didn't play along. He's just as stubborn and cocky as my brother sometimes. If he had, maybe things would be different.

You tried to protect him because you love him.

While that's true, it doesn't change the fact that I couldn't stop the ball from rolling down the hill and crashing into a tree. It didn't work. Better to keep my head down until his time is up. Then everything can go on the way it should.

What happened to the girl who could stand up for herself, who was confident and a ballbuster?

The baby kicks again, as if sending me a message.

"What is it?" I whisper. She kicks again and it becomes clear. She wants her mama to fight. Or at least, that's what I think she's trying to tell me. I rub my stomach. "Okay, baby, okay."

I put the car in gear and drive to the clubhouse, giving myself a pep talk the entire two minutes it takes to get there.

CHAPTER 21

MAGIC

"I've waited a week so when do we ride?"

I'm standing behind my chair, legs braced apart and arms over my chest. Today is supposed to be the day we plan our attack on Marlene and Cedric and I, for one, am ready. More than ready.

"Magic, sit down," Snow instructs. "Every man here knows what you want. You don't need to hover to make your position clear."

"If it's all the same to you, Prez, I'll stand." I bounce slightly on my feet, like a boxer gearing up to strike. "I'm too wired."

"Suit yourself. But remember where you are."

"Why don't we take a vote on whether or not we move today?" Duck suggests. "Maybe that will calm him down for a few minutes so we can actually discuss a plan."

"Fine. All in favor of moving today, raise your hand."

Every brother puts a hand up, and I add both of mine for good measure.

"Great." Snow faces me again. "That work for you, Magic?"

151

"Oh you know it does."

"Now that we know it'll be today, let's hash out a plan." Snow finally sits, but I remain standing. "The floor is open for discussion."

"We go to their house in Littleton, force our way in, kill them slowly, and get out."

"And deprive you of your time in the shed?" Toga asks. "You sure you want to give that up, Magic?"

"No. But I want them eliminated. It's already three years too late. Why drag it out?"

"Because the last time you went in and got out quickly, Cedric survived," Duck snaps. "We can't afford the same mistake."

"It wasn't a mistake!" I shout, anger roiling at being called out like this. "I did the job I was supposed to do."

"Yet here we are."

"Both of you shut up," Snow demands. "What's done is done. We're not here to hash out what happened back then."

"Maybe we should, Prez," Dip says and when I glare at him, he holds his hands up. "Look, I'm not saying we should put Magic on trial here, but I do think it can't hurt to figure out what went wrong. So we don't do it again."

"Nothing went wrong," I insist, unable to accept that I missed something. "At least, nothing I did. There had to have been someone else there who was able to get him out, or close by at least."

"Marlene?"

"That'd be my guess. No neighbors jumped to the rescue. And if it were firemen who saved him, don't you think there would have been more news coverage beyond just the fact that there was a fire?"

"True," Snow concedes. "And let's face it, Marlene is

shifty and resourceful. And she would do anything for her brother, including running into a burning house to save him."

"Great, we're agreed then? I didn't fuck up."

"Magic, no one ever said you fucked up. Shit happens. This is just a big, steaming pile of shit."

"Don't you think I know that?" I throw my hands up. "Do you seriously think I don't beat myself up every single second knowing that what I failed to do put Laney and my baby in jeopardy? I hate to break it to you, but there is *nothing* you can say or do that will make me feel worse than I already do."

"No one is trying to make you—"

The door opens, pulling everyone's attention in that direction. When I see Laney standing there, my jaw drops. I glance at Snow and see the fury that fills his eyes. What the fuck does she think she's doing?

"Sorry to interrupt guys," Laney says as she walks to stand at the head of the table. "But we need to talk."

"Laney, you need to leave," Snow says, rising from his chair. "Now."

He grips her upper arms and tries to turn her toward the door, but she doesn't budge. Instead, she yanks out of his hold and moves to stand next to me.

Damn, she's amazing.

"Duck, if someone asked you a year ago to describe me, what would you have said?"

Duke darts his gaze from her to Snow and back again. He opens his mouth several times before he's able to get any words out.

"Um, well, you're hot." Snow growls at Duck, but doesn't stop him from continuing. "Smart, independent, a little scary."

"Scary?"

"Yeah, ya know, because you never seem to buckle under pressure. No one ever gave you any shit. And the prospects? Man did you ever keep them in line. It was awesome to watch."

"Thank you, Duck. Now, how would you answer that same question today?" He averts his eyes. "You're not gonna hurt my feelings, Duck. It's okay."

"You've changed, Laney. Don't get me wrong, you're still sexy as hell." His eyes travel from her face to her stomach, and I clench my fists to keep from launching across the table and strangling him. "Even pregnant, you can light up a room. But you're more reserved. Softer maybe. I guess. I don't know." He shrugs, clearly uncomfortable. "You don't scare me anymore, I know that."

Laney leans as far across the table as her belly will allow and reaches for Duck's hand. "I love you too, D."

He squirms, but smiles. Then Laney straightens and turns to face Toga.

"How about you? How would you answer the same question?"

"Aw, Laney, why ya gotta put me in the spotlight?"

"Just answer me," she bites out.

"I guess I'd agree with Duck. You don't really stand up and fight anymore." He grins. "I miss that."

"Noted."

Laney turns to face me, her back to her brother. "And Magic, how would you answer those questions?"

"Laney," Snow barks. "Enough. I will not stand by and let you ma—"

Laney looks over her shoulder. "Shut up, Zeke," she snarls. "You're always talking. It's my turn."

Snow presses his lips together, but make no mistake, he's going to lose it the second she's out of the room.

"Magic?" Laney prods.

"You're all of the things Duck and Toga said... and so much more. You're beautiful, whether it's in your club party getup or sweats and a stained t-shirt. You're an amazing mother and little sister. You love with your whole heart, body, and soul. You stand up for yourself and those you count as family." I look around the room. "In other words, you've got all our backs, no matter what the cost. You're smart, strong, passionate. And you're also vulnerable, sweet, soft in all the best ways."

Laney's eyes shimmer and she clears her throat. "Do all of those apply to a year ago and today?"

"Yes. but..." I glance at Snow, who's skin is slowly returning to a state of normalcy. His anger is dissipating. "I don't know if it's the pregnancy making you careful, or everything that went down when we came clean, or what, but you tend to bow down a little more. There was a time you'd burst into your brother's house, consequences be damned, and read him the riot act. But now?" I shake my head. "Now I think you second-guess everything, no matter how strongly you feel about it."

Laney rises to her tiptoes and kisses my cheek. "I love you, Magic," she whispers in my ear.

"Are you finished?" Snow demands.

Laney whirls around and stomps toward her brother. "No, Zeke, I'm not done. How would you answer that question?"

"Laney, this is ridiculous. You know your place, you always have."

"That's just it, Zeke. Yes, as far as Satan's Legacy goes, I have a role, a place, and I get it. But Satan's Legacy doesn't define me like it does you. I'm not a member. I have no rights where the club is concerned." She waves a hand. "Oh, I know you preach respecting women and treating them like queens, which is great... when I'm on club time. But ninety percent of my life is just me being me. A mother, a sister, a girlfriend, a friend. Ninety percent of me doesn't have a damn thing to do with Satan's Legacy. That's something you should probably try to remember because I'm not going to sit idly by any longer and let you dictate my life."

Snow's eyes narrow. "I don't dictate your life, Laney. I do what I have to in order to keep you safe."

"Don't you get it?" she cries. "That's not your job. I'm not a teenager anymore, Zeke. I'm all grown up with a mind of my own, a life of my own. I stopped needing you to be a surrogate parent as soon as I turned eighteen. It's time to be my brother again and not my caretaker."

"I am your brother," Snow insists. "And a brother protects his sister. Aren't you going to teach Shiloh exactly that, to look out for his baby sister?" he asks, nodding to her stomach.

"Yeah, I am. But I'm also going to teach him to respect her, to be her biggest cheerleader and a shoulder to cry on when she needs one. I'm going to teach him that the best big brothers encourage their sisters to be strong and independent while he waits in the wings to catch her if she falls."

"I'm sorry to break up this whole family therapy session," Dip comments. "But Laney, why did you have to interrupt church for all this?"

Laney turns away from Snow and focuses on the rest of us around the table. "I'm sorry. This isn't exactly what I had in mind when I barged in here, but it's not—"

"Get to the point," Snow barks. "Why are you here?"

I take it as a step in the right direction that he doesn't demand she leave again.

Laney grins and cocks her head. "You mean you haven't figured it out yet?"

"If this is what we talked about earlier, I already told you no."

"And you don't have the right to do that."

"Excuse me? I'm the president. I have the right to do anything I fucking want."

"Zeke, I tried to do this the easy way, but you're putting me in a tough position." Snow glares at her as if daring her to make things more difficult. Apparently, she found her fighting spirit because she breaks out the big guns. "Are you forgetting bylaw forty-three? If I'm not mistaken, it gives the family of members the right to bring issues before the club for a vote, if such issues relate to the infringement of their rights. Oh, and let's not forget section B where it says that if the president refuses to hear a resident of the compound out, the resident may bypass him and go straight to the voting members."

Snow bristles. "I haven't forgotten. But it also states that the person with a grievance must submit a request to be heard at the next scheduled church session." He points his finger at her. "It doesn't give you the right to barge in here and take over an emergency session."

"This isn't an emergency session. It's been scheduled for a week!"

"And you haven't submitted the required request."

Laney stomps her foot. "You are such an asshole!"

"And you're a spoiled brat who thinks she can make demands and throw a tantrum like a child—"

"Stop it!" I shout, bringing my fists down on the table. "You're both acting like children. Snow, you refuse to hear

Laney out when it comes to things you don't agree with." I shift my gaze to Laney. "And you, you know the rules. I know you think you're doing the right thing. Hell, I admire you for it. But is this really how to go about this?"

"If it means getting you back, yes." She nods. "Do you really think it's in my nature to sit back and suck it up? Because if you do, maybe you don't know me as well as you think."

My shoulders slump. "No, Laney, I don't think it's in your nature. But I do think there's a time and place for this, and right now isn't it."

"It's exactly the place and time," she counters and faces the group. "I'm requesting a vote on lifting Magic's sanction for lying." Snow opens his mouth to speak, but she holds her hand up. "And before you say anything, I'll remind you that it's also infringing on my rights. Not only are you punishing Magic, but you're also dictating who I can date, who I can spend time with. Not to mention the punishment to our little girl." She runs her hand in circles over her belly. "You're denying her the right to have her father around for every single part of her life, even before she's born. I have to say, it scares me a little how much control the club will try to assert as she grows."

Pride wells in my heart for this woman. I knew she had that brass set tucked away in there.

Carnie stands up and leans on the table. "Prez, I hate to be the one to point out the obvious, but it seems we have a vote to take."

"Snow, c'mon, man," Duck says, rising and moving to stand next to him. "Are we really punishing him the way we should be? Laney has a point."

"Not you too," Snow complains. "We voted on his sentence as a club. It was unanimous."

"It was," Dip agrees, standing as well. "There is no doubt that Magic lied. And with the lie comes punishment. But does the punishment fit the crime? I'm not so sure. Fuck, I wasn't sure then either."

"Is this how you all feel?" Snow asks.

"I can't speak for everyone," Brady says. "But it's how I feel. I recommended a beat down at the first vote. I never really thought it was right to refuse to let them be together. You don't get to pick who you fall in love with, Prez. No one tried to stop you from seeing Sami."

"Laney did," Snow huffs.

"And I was doing then what I'm doing now. Standing up for what I thought was right." Laney's posture relaxes and her face softens. "Even I can admit when I'm wrong. I was so wrong about Sami and Lennox. They're amazing, and I love them both very much." She shoots me a quick glance and then returns her gaze to her brother. "Can you do the same?"

Snow takes a deep breath, as do I. The difference is, I hold mine in while he releases his.

"All in favor of ending Magic's sentence, effective immediately, raise your hand."

My head spins, and my heart pounds while I watch the vote take place.

One by one, my brothers raise their hands. Air rushes past my lips in relief. She did it. Laney managed to do the one thing I couldn't bring myself to even try. I'd accepted my fate, and really, it was almost over. And that's why she's stronger than I am.

Snow drops back into his chair. "Magic, you're no longer forbidden to see Laney." He darts his eyes back and forth between us. "But you both need to know this... I'm not okay with what you did. Not because it was the two of you, but because you lied. We don't have secrets in this family beyond club business."

Laney throws her arms around her brother and kisses his cheek. "Thank you, Zeke."

Then she runs toward me and wraps her arms around my neck as I lift her off her feet. Laney plants a kiss on my lips, and only when the cat calls begin do I pull away.

"You are amazing, Sweet Cheeks." I wink at her.

"No." She shakes her head. "*We* are."

CHAPTER 22

LANEY

"You okay?"

Magic lifts my hand from the center console and brings it to his lips. He's taking me to the doctor for the first time and, for some reason, I'm nervous. It also doesn't help that we just passed the accident site.

I smile at him. "I'm good."

"Laney, I know you better than you know yourself sometimes. You're not good. Talk to me."

I rest my elbow between us and my chin in my hand. *Talk to me.* It's such a simple request, one that was a normal, everyday occurrence. But now, it's going to take some getting used to again.

"It's just weird, ya know? Not only are you going with me to the doctor, but Snow knows about it. And not just because he ordered you to watch over me."

"To be fair, he did order me to go with you."

I flick my wrist. "That was just his way of giving us his blessing while not outright admitting he was wrong."

"Maybe."

"Are you worried about it?"

"No, not really."

"But a little bit?"

Magic shrugs. "A little."

I lean forward and press a kiss to his cheek. "Well, stop worrying. Snow doesn't do anything he doesn't want to do. I only moved things along."

"You really did put him in his place." He chuckles but keeps his eyes on the road. "The look on his face when you started quoting the bylaws... priceless."

"Yeah, well, he should've remembered our parents making both of us memorize them. We were raised in this club, and we had to know everything there was to know about it since Dad was the original president."

"Good point."

I laugh as I face forward and stare out the windshield. We've made it to a main road and the trees are starting to become sparse as we get closer to the city. Houses dot the landscape, making me fall into a trance as I watch them pass.

The rest of the drive is quiet, other than the music coming from the truck's speakers. I can't wait until I can get back on my Harley and ride next to Magic as the wind whips my hair and the air flows over my face. I miss that freedom, the thrill of it all.

Magic drives around the block several times before finding a spot to park. We walk to the office, his arm slung over my shoulders. This is new, at least out in public, and it's something I like... very much.

Before we walk through the door, I look over my shoulder. The hair on my arms is rising to attention, that sense that someone is watching me putting me on alert.

"What's wrong?" Magic asks, no doubt feeling my hesitation.

"Nothing." I look up at him and see the worry in his eyes. "Ya know that feeling you get like someone is watching you?" He nods. "I've got it."

Magic quickly scans our surroundings. Apparently satisfied that all is well, he gently pulls me through the doorway.

"We're fine. Besides, I'm here. No one can get to you."

I put one foot in front of another, willing myself to keep going and leave my fear at the door. I make it to the waiting room, but my nervous energy remains, riding me like a man rides a bull.

"Have a seat," Magic urges me into a chair along the wall. "I'll get you checked in."

He walks to the receptionist, answers a few questions and then returns to sit next to me. Magic lifts my hand and rests it in his lap, linking his fingers with mine.

"The last time I was in here, you found out you were pregnant," he says, a smile in his voice. "I can't wait to see our girl on the ultrasound."

"Uh-huh. Me either."

"And hear her heartbeat. I think that's what I'm looking forward to the most. Do you think we could..."

I don't hear the rest of his question. My ears start to ring, like an alarm alerting me to danger. I dart my eyes from one waiting patient to another, and then look at each staff member as if I can see through to their evil.

Something is wrong. I know it just like I know the sky is blue. The problem is, nothing appears off. Other than my racing heart and a gut feeling.

"Laney," a nurse calls as she holds the door to the exam rooms open with her back.

Magic and I stand to walk toward her, but I stop after a

few steps. Magic looks at me questioningly and I brush off the nerves.

Walk Laney. You're fine. Magic's here.

"If you'll follow me..."

The nurse leads us to a room at the end of the long hall. Magic sits in one of the blue plastic chairs while I sit on the exam table.

"I'm just gonna get your vitals," she says as she takes the blood pressure cuff from the hook on the wall. It constricts my arm so tightly I can practically feel my veins pulse against it. "Hmm. Your blood pressure is high." She makes a note in my chart on the counter. "Any additional stress since the accident?"

I shake my head and try to swallow around the lump in my throat. "Can you get the doctor please?" I ask. "I'm not feeling so good."

Magic comes to stand next to me and rubs a hand over my back. "Laney, what's wrong?"

I press a hand to my chest. "Heart's racing, dizzy..." I try to bring Magic into focus but all I see is a blurry blob.

The nurse runs out into the hall, and I hear her yell, although I can't make out her words. I hope whatever they are, they get the attention of the doctor.

I grip the edge of the table, thinking it will somehow ground me. It helps a little, but not enough. The room still spins, and with each inhale, air is getting harder and harder to suck in.

"Magic..." I lick my lips. "Something's wrong."

"Ah, Laney," Dr. Dryer's voice booms through the thickening fog. "Are you having trouble breathing?" I nod and she places an oxygen mask over my mouth and nose. "Any chest pains?" she asks as she places a stethoscope over my heart. "Laney, I need you to listen to me, okay?" More nodding. "I'm pretty sure you're having a panic attack. We need to get your heart rate slowed down and your breathing evened out."

Dr. Dryer talks me through a series of breathing exercises, her voice remaining even and calm the entire time. When she's done, my vision is clear, and I don't feel like my mind is spinning out of control. I can breathe without the oxygen, and my heart isn't threatening to beat out of my chest.

My blood pressure is checked again.

"That's much better," the doctor says, a smile on her face. "It's not back to normal, but within an acceptable range."

"Thank God," Magic says on a sigh. "Shit, Laney, don't scare me like that again."

"I'm sorry. I was scared too."

He cups my cheeks and kisses me, deeply. For a moment, I forget we're at the doctor's office. It's been a long time since he's kissed me like that.

Dr. Dryer clears her throat, and we jump apart. "Before you get her too worked up again, I'd like to have some tests run. I've already had the nurse call for an ambulance to transport you to the hospital."

"Tests?" I ask, worried again. "I thought it was just a panic attack."

"And I can take her to the hospital. No ambulance," Magic insists.

"Let's take one concern at a time." Dr. Dryer sits on the rolling stool. "Laney, I do think it was a panic attack. But I'd rather play things on the safe side, just to be sure. The hospital has the ability to run more tests than I do. I will meet you there as soon as I can to oversee your care. Hopefully, you'll go home tonight."

"Hopefully?" I chew on my bottom lip. "There's a chance I won't?"

"One step at a time, okay?" She rests her hand on my knee. "If, on the off chance it's more than a panic attack, you may need to stay overnight for monitoring. But we'll cross that bridge if and when we have to."

She swivels to address Magic. "As for you taking her to the hospital... I know you can. But policy dictates that she be transported by ambulance for monitoring purposes."

"I can monitor her," Magic insists.

"Can you?" When he nods, she holds a hand up. "You just experienced the same thing she did. It's traumatic to see a loved one have an episode where you're essentially hopeless. I need you to focus on getting yourself there so you can be by her side. Trust us to get her there safely. Can you do that for me?"

"I'll ride with her, then. I'll deal with my truck later."

"I'm sorry," Dr. Dryer says, shaking her head. "I know you two are close, probably closer than most married couples. But it's family only in the ambulance. I simply can't let you go with her."

Magic lifts his eyes to mine, silently begging me to tell her she's wrong, to side with him.

"She's right, Magic. I can feel your hands shaking just sitting here. I'll be fine."

Magic addresses the doctor again. "Can you give us a minute?"

"Absolutely. I'll go check on the status of the ambulance and come back in a few minutes."

When she's out of the room, Magic wastes no time.

"I don't like this. What if they're out there, watching? I can't let you out of my sight."

"Yes, you can. And you will. It's what, a few blocks to the hospital? I'll be fine."

Magic takes a minute before responding. "You have your cell, right? So you can call me if anything goes wrong?"

"I do."

"Promise me you'll use it, Laney. I need to know that you'll call, even if it's just because something feels off."

"I promise."

I want to tell him that nothing will go wrong, that I'll be in an ambulance, safe from the outside world. But he's going to worry anyway so my promise is easier than the argument.

Finally, Magic gives a curt nod. "Fine. I'll meet you there."

CHAPTER 23

MAGIC

I race to the hospital, weaving my truck in and out of traffic like a mad man. The second Laney was loaded into the ambulance, I took off for my truck and didn't look back. I need to beat her there, so she sees my face as soon as she's brought in. I tell myself I'm doing this for her, but the truth is, it's for me.

When I reach the parking lot, I find the first available space and slam the truck into park. I'm out of the vehicle and running toward the door before I even have a chance to blink.

"There's an ambulance coming in with my girlfriend. Are they here yet?"

The receptionist smiles at me. "Welcome to UCHealth, sir. If you'll please wait your turn." She points to the line of fidgety people now standing behind me.

"Lady, I'm here, it's my fucking turn. Did the ambulance with Laney Barnes arrive yet?"

"Sir, I'll have to call security if you don't step back and wait your turn."

I smack my hands on the counter. "Call security. Do

168

what you have to do." I point to the Devil patch on my cut. "But first, Laney Barnes, ambulance... is it here?"

Her smile disappears and her eyes widen. "Oh, I'm sorry sir. I didn't realize." She sits down and starts tapping away at her keyboard. "Laney Barnes, Laney Barnes... Oh, here she is. It seems the ambulance hasn't arrived yet. If you'll have a seat, I'll be sure to let you know the moment it does."

"That won't be necessary. Just tell me where she'll be brought in. I'll wait there."

"I'm afraid I can't—" She presses her lips together when I point to my patch again. Then she extends her hand to indicate the door to the right of her desk. "I'll open the door for you. You'll go to the end of the hall and take a right. The entrance she'll be brought in through will be at the end of that corridor."

"Thank you."

I don't even let the door open all the way before I'm sliding past it. When I reach the last hall, I see a patient being wheeled in on a gurney. I rush forward, but before I get to it, I can see it's not Laney. Flattening myself against the wall, I stay out of their way.

While I wait, I send a text to Snow to give him an update. I tell him about the panic attack and the doctor wanting to run more tests. I tell him she's on her way to the hospital and that I'll let him know when I know more.

Within seconds of hitting send, my phone rings.

"She's fine, Snow," I say instead of my usual greeting.

"She better be."

"All of her vitals were brought back into stable range at the doctor's office. Dr. Dryer wanted to be sure it wasn't more than a panic attack, so Laney is being transported here to the hospital. I'm waiting by the ambulance entrance now."

"You're not with her?" he growls into the line.

I knew this would be a sticking point. As it is with me.

"I wasn't exactly given a choice. It was the policy of the doctor's office that she be transported by ambulance."

"Again, why aren't you with her?"

"Bro, what was I supposed to do, take the ambulance hostage and drive it myself?"

"Don't be stupid," he snaps. "I'm sure you could have found a way to convince the doctor you needed to stay with her."

"I tried," I insist. "Short of threatening the good doc with a gun, which I thought was probably not the best idea considering she's the woman taking care of the mother of my child, there was nothing."

"Fine. But the second she gets there, you—"

My phone dings with a text notification. "Hang on a sec."

I pull my phone away from my ear and look at the text. My blood boils. It's from Laney and all it says is '911'.

"Snow, get everyone here," I bark as I take off back toward the reception area. "Laney just texted me 911. I'll meet you in the parking lot of UCHeatlh."

I disconnect the call and run through the halls and out the door. The receptionist calls out to me, but I don't stop. Not for her, not for anything. When I make it to my truck, I punch in the speed dial for Laney and bring the phone back up to my ear.

Nothing. She doesn't answer. I call again and again, praying each time will be different.

"You've reached Laney. I can't come to the—"

I stab the disconnect button and decide to try a text. If she can't answer the phone, I'm guessing she won't be able to respond to a text, but it's worth a shot.

Me: Call me!

A few tense moments go by but my cell dings with a notification.

Laney: Laney can't come to the phone right now. But I'd be happy to give her a message.

Me: Who is this?

Laney: Who the fuck do you think?

Me: Cedric

Laney: It's so good to chat with you again, Magic. I hated the way we left things last time.

My hands shake as I stare at the words. Rage builds beneath the surface, until I'm left squeezing my phone almost to the point of breaking.

Laney: I'm surprised you don't have anything to say.

Me: I've got plenty to say. And you'll listen to every word when I find you.

Laney: Better make it quick. Our girls don't have much time.

I raise my arm to throw my phone across the lot but freeze when I hear the rumble of Harleys. I step onto the running board of the truck and look over the other parked vehicles. A pack of bikes enter the lot, Snow leading the pack. I wave them over to my location.

"Where is she?" Snow demands after he parks.

"Cedric's got her."

I hand him my cell so he can see the texts. Before he's done, the cell dings again.

"He's texting again," Snow says and then reads the message aloud. "'I see the cavalry has arrived'."

"Motherfucker's watching us?" Duck turns in circles to see if he can spot him. "Where the hell is he?"

"More importantly, how did he get to her?" Snow glares at me. "The only time she was out of your sight was in the..."

"Ambulance," we both say in unison.

"Toga, call Brady and have him dig into employee records for all ambulance providers that contract with UCHealth," Snow demands. "The rest of us, mount back up. We're headed to Littleton a little earlier than we planned."

"Ya think he's stupid enough to go back to the house with her?" Dip asks, clearly unconvinced.

"No," Snow admits. "But I think he and Marlene are smart enough to have separate roles in this whole thing. Hopefully, her role keeps her at the house."

"And if it doesn't?" I ask. "We could show up there and find the house empty. Then what?"

"Let's hope we don't hav—" Snow's cell rings. He glances at the screen and then answers. "Brady, whatcha got for me?" Snow puts the phone on speaker so we can hear.

"There's a Cecil Tate that drives an ambulance. He's on the schedule for today and got dispatched to Dr. Dryer's office at the same time Laney was there. It has to be Cedric."

"Ya think?" Snow's comment is sarcastic, and no doubt fueled by fury and fear. "Any way to tap into the ambulance GPS and find out where they are?"

"I tried. The GPS has been disabled. The last location it registered was the same street the hospital is on, about five minutes ago."

"Anything on Marlene?"

"No. Nothing on her or Linda Tate."

"Okay, thanks Brady. Stay by the phone in case we need you."

"You got it, Prez."

The call is disconnected. "Looks like we're still going to Littleton. Toga and Dip, you two are with me. Duck and Carnie, you stay here with Magic until we get a better location on Laney." Snow looks to the others, patched members and prospects. "The rest of you, divide and conquer. Start riding through Denver, see if you can find the ambulance or Laney. You find something, you report it to me immediately." He glances at me. "Report it to Magic, as well. Neither one of us is to be kept out of the loop on anything. Got it?"

"Got it."

"Yes, sir."

"You can count on us."

Snow rests his hand on my shoulder. "We're going to bring them home, Magic."

And if we don't?

He gives me a reassuring squeeze. "You've got my word on that."

CHAPTER 24
LANEY

T bounce on the back seat with every pothole that is hit.

"Can't you dodge those?"

Cedric looks at me in the rearview mirror and smirks. "I'm sorry the travel accommodations aren't up to your standards, your highness."

"It's your cloth seats that will suffer." I shrug. "No skin off my back if they end up soiled with piss."

I've had to pee for the last hour. One of the downsides to being pregnant... the constant need to urinate. I'd planned on asking to go as soon as I reached the hospital, but that never happened. As soon as the ambulance pulled away from the doctor's office, Cedric revealed himself as the driver. He drove around for a while until pulling into a parking lot for an abandoned building, and we switched cars. The paramedic was paid off to keep his mouth shut, if the wad of cash Cedric handed him is any indication.

Cedric takes a sharp right turn sending me toward the middle of the seat. He pulls to the side of the road and throws the car in park before twisting in his seat. Then he braces his arm on the headrest across from him and that's when I see them... scars. He's wearing a long-sleeved shirt and jacket, so they've been hidden until now.

You might not have killed him, Magic, but you definitely left him a gruesome calling card.

"There's no time to empty your bladder." He reaches to the passenger seat and lifts a bottle. "If you gotta go, use this." He tosses it at me.

I eye the bottle skeptically. "In case you missed the memo, I can't aim like you can."

"Ya know, for someone who's being kidnapped, your attitude has a lot to be desired. But you're forgetting one thing, baby doll." His grin turns sinister. "I'm in charge and you're in cuffs."

How could I forget? They're digging into my wrists.

"I don't want to have to hurt you..." He nods at my stomach. "... or the brat. But if duty calls, I'm prepared."

He reaches into his inside jacket pocket, and a syringe flashes in the sunlight when he brings his hand back into view. I instinctively try to put my hands on my stomach, but the handcuffs hold me back. I keep pulling against them, over and over, until I feel a small trickle of blood run down my hand.

"You'll pay for this, Cedric," I seethe, baring my teeth.

"Like I did last time?" he taunts.

Slamming back against the seat, I shut up and quit struggling. Cedric clearly takes that as a sign of my giving up, but it's the furthest thing from it. Laney Barnes doesn't give up. She gets smart.

He turns around and shifts into drive but before he can pull away from the curb, his cell phone rings. Or is it mine? I don't know because he has both.

"What?" he barks into the phone. I glare at the back of

his head, silently demanding he put it on speaker, but he doesn't. "Yeah, I told you, piece of cake." He pauses to listen. "No, not yet. Satan's Legacy rallied the troops so we can't come to the house." He's shaking his head, and I can't help but wonder if somehow, his plan is going wrong. "Marlene… Marlene!" he shouts. "Shut up!… thank you. Now listen, you need to get out of there before they show up at the house. No, I don't know for sure, but I wouldn't put it past them." Cedric leans his head back against the seat and sighs. "Fine, do what you want," he spits out. "I'm going to the campground."

He disconnects the call and toss his phone to join mine on the passenger seat. So, he's taking me to a campground? If it were summer, I'd be happy about that because there'd likely be too many people around for him to kill me. But in the fall, after we've already had our first snow? My chances of survival just went down.

I remain quiet while he pulls into traffic and continues down the street. When he reaches the traffic light, he turns left to head out of the city. My bladder is screaming at me, and I endure it until I can't any longer.

"I really do have to pee," I say quietly.

"There's a McDonald's up a little ways. We'll stop there." He lifts the syringe so I can see it again. "But no funny business."

Yeah, right. He's delusional if he really thinks his threat is going to stop me from trying to escape.

"No funny business," I agree.

The golden arches come into view and Cedric turns into the parking lot. He parks the car and climbs out of the front seat. It crosses my mind to kick him in the chest when he opens my door, but I can't get into position fast enough.

"Come on," he says as he watches our surroundings.

I scoot to the door and swing my legs out. My hands are behind my back, so it's not easy, especially being almost seven months pregnant. Cedric hauls me out of the car and pushes me against the side.

"You're gonna go in with a smile on your face, walk straight to the bathroom and then right back here when you're done. Got it?"

"Yeah, got it." I twist slightly. "What about the cuffs?"

He unlocks them with a key he takes from his pocket. My skin pricks as feeling returns. Cedric hands me a balled-up tissue.

"Here, wipe off the blood."

I glance at the tissue and wrinkle my nose. No way am I rubbing his snot on my broken skin.

"It's clean," he snaps, shoving the tissue against my chest.

I quickly wipe away the blood and then stretch my sleeves to cover the small wound. Sure, I could leave it uncovered and hope someone sees it, but I need to be careful to not tip off Cedric to anything suspicious.

"Let's go."

He places his arm around my lower back and guides me to the door. Disgust ripples through me at his touch. Before the door even closes behind us, he's turning toward the bathrooms. I survey the restaurant and hope flares. It's full. But that hope is quickly dashed when I see the number of children. I count ten.

You can't put them in jeopardy.

Being a mother has its drawbacks, I guess. I have a conscience and couldn't possibly do anything that could end up harming a child.

Feeling defeated, I hand my head and force myself to focus on something I can do. I can go pee, so I don't feel like I'm going to drown in fluid. Maybe then I can focus on escaping.

After relieving myself, I open the bathroom door to find Cedric standing next to it. He looks nervous, and he should. He wraps his arm around me again and we start walking toward the exit.

When he opens the door, he steps aside for a woman who's entering. I don't recognize her at first, but then she lifts her head.

Heather!

She recognizes me too and throws her arms around me in a hug.

"Girl, I've missed you," she says when she steps back. "I haven't seen you around any parties lately."

I pat my stomach as if that says it all. "Thought it would be a little weird," I lie.

As if just noticing Cedric, Heather's eyes focus on him. She sticks her hand out, giving him no choice but to shake it. "Hi, I'm Heather." She gives him a moment to respond in kind, but he says nothing. When she pulls her hand back, her narrowed eyes dart to me. "Well, you sure know how to pick 'em, Laney."

"You'll have to forgive him. We're late for our check in at the campground, and he's pissed because we had to stop for me to pee."

Cedric pinches my back, the only thing he can do, without drawing attention from other diners, to show his rage at me having revealed part of his plan.

"Since when do you camp?" Heather asks, her brow furrowing.

C'mon, Heather. You have to know something isn't right here.

I nod toward Cedric. "He thought it would be a good time to try new things. With the baby coming, it'll be hard to do for a while."

"Makes sense." Heather winks at me. "Gotta please our men, am I right?"

No! He's not my man. He's my captor.

"You got that right."

"We should probably get going," Cedric says, displeasure apparent in his tone. "We're late enough."

"Well, don't let me keep you."

Cedric immediately starts guiding me through the door, but Heather stops us and grabs my arm.

"Laney, I almost forgot..." I twist to look at her and it's perfect because now Cedric can't see my face.

"Yes?" I ask, and then I mouth the word 'help'.

She drops my arm. "Ya know what? It can wait. Give me a call when you get back. Maybe we can get together?"

"I'll do that." I mouth the word 'help' again for good measure. "See ya."

Cedric practically drags me away from her then. I can feel her eyes on me the entire way to the car but when I look back, I don't see her.

"What the fuck was that?" Cedric barks out as he puts the cuffs back on me and shoves me into the car.

"What?" I ask innocently. "I don't control who goes to McDonald's, Cedric. Heather's a friend and I couldn't exactly ignore her. That would look suspicious."

"You told her we were going camping." His face is red, hard, full of rage.

"What was I supposed to do? Tell her I was headed

179

home? She's dating our VP and if she goes to the club and I'm not there, she'd know something was up."

"You better be right about her. If she blabs, her death will be on your head."

Oh, she's gonna blab. Big time. And then it will be your death on my head, and I'm perfectly fine with that.

"She won't say anything. Heather will be too focused on Duck to even remember seeing me."

CHAPTER 25
MAGIC

"What is taking them so long?"

I'm leaning against my truck, arms crossed over my chest. I feel helpless just sitting here. Laney is out there somewhere, and she's counting on me to find her.

"Bro, we'll hear from them soon. Maybe they're interrogating Marlene and will call—" Duck's phone rings. "Speak of the devil." He lifts it to his ear. "Yo." He pauses and then grins. "Oh, hey Heather. I'm a little…" His words trail off as he listens, and his face hardens. "Hold on, I'm gonna put you on speaker." He holds his phone out, face up, so Carnie and I can hear. "Say everything again."

"I think Laney's in trouble. I mean, she didn't say she was, but the whole situation was weird."

"You saw Laney?" I ask.

"Well, yeah. At the McDonald's on Colfax." Heather takes a deep breath and sighs. "Anyway, she was with some guy. I didn't get his name though. And she said they were going camping."

"Laney doesn't camp," Carnie says.

"No shit," Heather snaps. "Sorry. I just got a really bad vibe. And as they were leaving, she mouthed the word 'help' to me... twice."

"Anything else you can tell us?" Duck asks gently. "Anything at all?"

"Not really. The guy was average height and build. Sandy blond hair." The sound of snapping fingers comes through the line. "Oh, and he had scars. Like he'd been burnt or something. I noticed them when he reached for the door and his jacket slid up."

"That's Cedric alright." I run a hand through my hair. "Did she look hurt in any way?"

"Not that I could tell," Heather states. "More like pissed off. It struck me as odd that she was with another guy. What with Magic being the baby Daddy and his sanction being lifted early."

I glare at Duck and growl. He lowers his head but not in time to hide his grin.

"Heather, I need you to go to the compound," Duck tells her. "I don't think Cedric, or his sister, would try anything with you, but better safe than sorry. I'll call Brady and have him move everyone underground. When you get there, use the entrance from my basement, okay?"

"Okay, if you think it's necessary."

"I'm probably overreacting, to be honest." Duck lifts a finger to his lips, so Carnie and I don't contradict him. "But if anything happened to you, or anyone else at the compound, and I didn't try to prevent it, I'd never be able to live with myself."

I grab the phone from Duck and lift it close to my face. "We gotta go, Heather. Thanks for calling."

I disconnect the call and shove the cell into Duck's chest. "We need to focus."

MAGIC'S TORMENT

"Did you have to hang up on her?"

"You were dragging it out," I grit out. "Laney's life is on the line. Forgive me if I want to move things along so we can actually find her."

"Hey, chuckleheads." Carnie thrusts his cell phone in between Duck and me. "Take a look at this."

He proceeds to point to the McDonald's where Heather saw Laney and then trace his finger on the tiny map until he lands on Cherry Creek State Park.

"Laney said they were going camping. That McDonald's is right by Interstate 25, which leads to the state park. And if you'll notice, it's not far from Littleton. It has to be where Cedric is taking her."

We all look at the map, zoomed in and zoomed out, to try and find any alternatives that make sense. Nothing jumps out to me as being a viable option, unless the whole camping thing was a decoy on Cedric's part. But no, it fits with him and Marlene bouncing from campground to campground before buying the house in Littleton.

I yank open the door to my truck and jump in. "Make whatever phone calls you have to make but I'm not sticking around and wasting more time."

I turn the key, and the engine roars to life. Carnie and Duck protest, but I slam the door, drowning them out. I peel out of the parking space, not giving a damn if they follow or not. I glance in my rearview mirror and see Duck on his phone as he straddles his Harley. Carnie is on his as well, waiting for instructions.

"I'm coming, Laney," I say. "Hang in there a little longer.

I hear her voice in my head, telling me everything will be okay, that she's holding her own. I hope my imagination is right.

I take the on ramp for the interstate and stomp on the

gas. I weave in and out of traffic, dodging any vehicle that will slow me down. I don't have time for that shit.

My cell phone dings with a notification, and I glance at it. It's a text from Snow. I slide my finger on the screen to open it and dart my eyes back and forth between my phone and the road so I can read it.

Snow: House empty. Meet u at park entrance. Don't do anything stupid.

I lift my head and slam on the brakes just before rear ending a semi. My heart is pounding so hard my ears feel like they're going to explode off my head. My fingers tighten around the steering wheel. My knuckles turn white, and only when I'm sure they're on the verge of breaking do I loosen my grip.

Pull it together. You've gotta be ready for anything.

If I can't even handle traffic, how am I going to rescue Laney? I don't let up on the speed, but I do shove my phone in my pocket and ignore every notification until I reach the park.

At the entrance, I let off the gas, slowing down to pull over, then decide against it. Fuck Snow and his instructions. This is Laney and I'm not waiting.

I barrel past the guard house, ignoring the man waving his hands for me to stop so I can pay the entry fee.

I'll get ya on the way out, buddy.

There are several camping sites in the state park, and I drive through every one. I have no idea if they're still in the ambulance, but my gut tells me they aren't. Which leaves almost any other vehicle as an option. Is Cedric stupid enough to drive the green Jeep? Will they be in a tent or a cabin? Does Cedric have a camper we don't know about?

It takes what feels like forever to search the entire park, but not knowing what I'm looking for slows me down considerably.

I slam my fist into the horn, and it blasts a short bleat, as I leave the latest campground without finding Laney or Cedric. I navigate the narrow road to the next one, Cottonwood Grove Camping Loop. That and two others are the only ones left.

I turn onto the dirt road that leads to the site and slow down when I spot two vehicles parked next to a small camper: a gold Buick Century and a dark green Jeep Cherokee. There are fresh tire tracks behind both and footprints leading to the side door of the camper.

Got ya!

I continue driving past, not wanting to tip Cedric off to my presence. If I spook him, Laney suffers. Besides, he's probably not alone, given the second vehicle. No, I've gotta be smart about this.

Turning out of the loop, I pull my truck off the narrow road to park it near a copse of trees. I fling my door open and hop down, careful not to slam the door too hard behind me. I double check that I have my knife and my gun, although I know I do. I never leave home without them.

Sticking to the tree line, I make my way back to the camper. There weren't any other people at this particular site, but that doesn't mean there won't be. The more I can make myself a ghost, the better.

As I creep up toward the back of the camper, I hear raised voices. I'm able to identify them as Cedric and Marlene and judging by the words Cedric is spewing, Marlene fucked up.

"He was your responsibility!" he yells. "All I was supposed to do was grab this bitch. Shiloh is on you."

"I went to the school," Marlene shouts back. "She pulled him after shit went down with you three years ago. If you'd have done your research like I told you to, this could all be avoided."

I pull my cell out of my cut and press the volume button until I know it will be silent. Then I open my messages and tap on my previous exchange with Sami.

Me: Shiloh still with you?

Three bouncing dots appear as she responds.

Sami: Yeah. Underground. He's fine.

I breathe a sigh of relief and tune my ears back to the shouting match going on beyond the pitiful walls. I'd try to see inside, but all the ugly curtains are drawn. I wish Laney would say something, just so I know she's okay, but with the arguing going on, I don't blame her for staying quiet.

Time to get creative.

CHAPTER 26
LANEY

"Who gives a fuck about the boy?"

The crack of Marlene's palm on Cedric's cheek seems shrill in the tiny space. She leans in as she grabs his hair to make him face her. Her other hand remains at her side, holding the gun she arrived with.

"He's your son," she says, spittle flying from her lips. "He belongs with you."

"No, you want him," Cedric counters. "I couldn't give two shits about the kid." He nods at me. "She's probably poisoned him against me anyway."

No, I haven't. All he knows is you died. Ironic, really, that I chose to let him think you were a good person.

"Listen, you twit," Marlene says in a tight voice, raising her gun to point it at his chin. "I didn't pull you out of that fire just to let you make stupid decisions. I did it so we could get your son back. We've spent years planning this, and I'll be damned if you're gonna fuck it up."

"What are you suggesting?" He shoves his way free of her. "Because there's no way I'm going to that compound to get him. You know as well as I do that he's probably under lock and key by now."

"He's right, Marlene." When she turns to me and gives me a 'how dare you speak' look, I don't let it intimidate me. I try to ignore the weapon now pointed at my head, as well. "You know Satan's Legacy has already gone underground. And all the entrances are probably guarded by now. You can't get to Shiloh."

She dated Snow for a little over a year and I know she's been there when we've been shuffled below ground. This shouldn't be news to her.

"Like you'd tell us the truth now," Marlene huffs out.

"Believe what you want." I shrug as if this is the most normal conversation in the history of conversations. "But why would I lie? Once you realize I am telling you the truth, your focus will be on me." I tug on the ropes binding me to the chair. "I can't exactly defend myself or get away."

Marlene lunges forward and yanks my head back by my hair. She puts the gun up to my chin this time, and the cold metal sends terror though my veins. But I don't dare let that show.

"I know what you're doing," she accuses. "You're trying to get in my head, pin me and Cedric against each other or whatever. But it's not gonna work!"

"Stop it, Marlene!" Cedric walks toward her as he yells. "We don't have time for this shit. No doubt someone's been to the house already and found it empty. We need to figure out a different plan, since you veered off course."

Marlene's shoulders slump, but her face remains cold and calculated. "What do you—"

A knock on the door startles them, both jumping slightly at the sound. They exchange a look and then turn their attention on me.

"What have you done?" Cedric asks in a hushed tone.

I don't bother being quiet. I need whoever is at the door to know this camper isn't empty.

"Nothing. You've been with me the entire time and you took my phone. What could I have possibly done?"

Another knock comes, louder this time.

"Park Ranger," the person says with a southern drawl. I recognize Magic's voice right away, but my two bumbling buddies don't seem to. "Open the door please."

Marlene presses her gun to Cedric's side and lifts a finger to her lips. "Don't say a word."

"I can hear you in there," Magic says. "Look, I just need to show you a picture of a dog, see if you've seen it. Apparently, she's skittish." He chuckles to sell his lie. "Some campers on another loop said she got spooked by a passing vehicle and slipped her collar."

"There's no dog here," Cedric responds.

Marlene elbows him in the stomach and he doubles over. With her attention on her brother, I take a chance.

"No, remember we saw that border collie earlier?" I say, as if just conversing with Cedric. "Maybe we should look at the picture, just to be sure it's not the same dog."

Cedric glares at me, but resignation flashes in his eyes. There's no way out of this now. One of them has to let the *park ranger* in. He walks to the door and opens it.

The barrel of a gun is pressed against his forehead as he's shoved backward into Marlene, knocking her to the floor and sending her weapon sliding across the linoleum. Magic clears the door and stomps a booted foot into her back to keep her from moving. His eyes dart to me.

"Hey, Sweet Cheeks. You doing okay?"

I tug on my restraints. "Other than this, yeah."

189

Magic bends to grab his knife and reaches over to slice one hand free. He hands me the blade so I can get the rest.

"I take it Heather called?" I try to remain calm and keep things light, but my hands are shaking. The adrenaline and all my bravado are fading now that Magic's here.

"Yep." I hand him the rope after freeing myself. He begins to tie up Cedric, as he continues. "It's pure dumb luck that you ran into her."

"Ouch," Cedric complains. "Does it have to be so tight?"

"I wouldn't worry about the rope," Magic seethes as he cinches it tighter. "This is nothing compared to what you've got waiting for you." He turns his head to look at me. "Take that other rope and tie her up," he instructs as he nods at Marlene.

"Why can't we just kill them?" I ask, frustrated that he's not ending it here and now.

"They're gonna die, but not here. Too much out of our control here."

"If you say so."

I drop to my knees next to the woman and yank her arms behind her back. I wind the rope around her wrists and tie them as tight as I can.

"I told you to meet at the park entrance."

Bad guys secure, both Magic and I whirl around toward the door. Snow is standing just inside the threshold, Duck, Carnie, Toga, and Dip behind him. I race to him and throw my arms around his neck. He lifts me off the floor in a big hug. I bury my head in the crook of his neck and hold on tight.

"You're okay now, Laney," Snow croons.

His voice is soothing somehow, but I know he's angry. Beyond angry is probably more accurate. When he sets me

MAGIC'S TORMENT

down, his face is back to a stone mask as he addresses Magic again.

"You're lucky your recklessness is ending on a good note." He darts his gaze between Marlene and Cedric. "Surely you can do better than this, Magic. Tying them up is a little juvenile, don't you think?"

Magic pretends to consider it for a moment and taps his chin in the process. "Now that you mention it, there is somewhere I'd like to take them."

"Wherever it is," I say. "I'm going too."

Snow and Magic exchange a look then Magic raises a shoulder.

"I'm okay with it, if you are," he says to my brother.

Snow looks at me. "Laney, it's not anywhere pleasant. Besides, don't you think you should get checked out at the hospital? You were supposed to be going there before this motherfucker got in the way." He points at Cedric.

"I can handle it," I insist. "Magic's the Enforcer so I'm well aware that things will get ugly. In fact, I'm counting on it."

"You should go to the hospital first," Carnie says, adding in his two cents. "Just to be safe."

"Prez, if you can handle getting these two back to the compound, I'll take Laney to the hospital." Magic steps forward and grabs my hand. "They can sit on ice until we get there. And then we'll make them pay... together."

Snow runs his hand through his beard, and I fully expect him to say no. How quickly he's forgetting about this morning when I told him I'm a big girl and can take care of myself.

"Fine. Laney comes first," he finally says, and I release the breath I didn't know I was holding. "Her and the baby... and Shiloh."

I can tell he's not just referring to the topic at hand, but he's putting Magic on notice of how he's to prioritize moving forward. And I have to say, I'm a little surprised. The club is supposed to come first.

Magic grins.

"Always, brother. Always."

CHAPTER 27

LANEY

"Here, take this."

I stare at the torch Magic is holding in front of me. We got back to the compound about an hour ago, and Magic suggested we check on Shiloh before coming to his house to get his 'tools'. Shiloh was fine. Excited in fact, because he and Lennox were allowed to run the tunnels that are under the compound. Brady stayed with them, of course, but the boys always turn a retreat underground like an adventure.

"Laney?" I lift my head. "If you don't want to do this, it's okay. You can go get Shiloh from Snow and Sami and have a movie night with him."

I shake my head, trying to dispel the hesitation. I'm not afraid of this, whatever this is. I can handle blood and gore, even when I'm the one causing it. But I'd be lying if I didn't say I wasn't a little worried about my blood pressure topping the charts again.

At the hospital, all the tests Dr. Dryer ordered were finally conducted. They confirmed the panic attack earlier and then sent me home with instructions to 'take it easy' and 'avoid stressful situations'.

My whole life is a stressful situation. I'm a single mother, the sister of an MC president, and the pregnant girlfriend of their enforcer. Yeah, avoid stress my ass.

I contemplate taking Magic up on his offer, but as soon as I do, I feel my heart rate climb. No, I have to do this. When it's done, I can work on that whole stress thing. And helping Magic get rid of Cedric and Marlene is a damn good start.

I grab the torch from his hand. It's not big or cumbersome, more like a giant lighter on steroids. I like it. Magic turns to walk back to the safe tucked into the wall behind his dresser. He grabs a machete and flips it in his hand a few times.

With his back to me, I let my eyes wander. His shoulders are broad, his biceps bulging. His back is straight, so I know he's confident about what we're going to do. Tendrils of yearning curl around me like thick smoke, threatening to pull me under until I'm a horny pile of hormones.

Fuck, I missed him. In every single way.

I vow to myself that when this is over, we're going to celebrate in the most carnal fashion possible.

Magic turns and takes in my hooded eyes, my tense posture, my clenching and unclenching hands. He stalks toward me and grabs my arms to guide me toward the bed. I want him to keep going, need him to.

But business first.

"Trust me, Magic," I say, grabbing him through his jeans. "This will happen. As soon as we're done with them." I run a finger up his chest, over his chin, and past his lips. When he swirls his tongue around it, I almost cave. But I stand strong. "It'll be worth the wait. I promise."

He quickly releases my finger and steps back. Magic adjusts himself and rage enters his features. The grin that tugs his lips carries no remnant of the lust he was feeling a second ago. He's put his game face on.

"Let's do this."

Magic grabs my hand and leads me out of the house and toward the woods at the back of the property.

"Where are we going?" I ask.

"You'll see."

I dig in my feet. "Magic, there's nothing back here." A thought occurs to me. "Please tell me they aren't just tied to a tree or something. Because they've already proven good at escaping."

Magic throws his head back and laughs. It bothers me, because it feels like he's laughing at me, but I push away my annoyance.

"Sweet Cheeks, you have so much to learn." He leans forward and presses a kiss to my forehead. "I promise you, they aren't tied to a tree. And they sure as shit aren't escaping."

"You're sure?"

"Laney, do you trust me?"

I balk at the question. "Of course I do."

"Then act like it."

With that, he swats my ass and then continues to lead me further into the woods. It's dark out and I stumble over a few fallen branches, but Magic keeps me from falling. We seem to walk forever, but it's probably only a few hundred yards. That's when I see it, a ramshackle shed.

"Ah, the promised land," Magic says, giddiness entering his tone.

I narrow my eyes. "That thing?" I ask, nodding toward the structure. "That would blow over in a gentle breeze."

"Which is exactly the kind of vibe it's supposed to put off." He tugs me forward, picking up the pace. "C'mon."

We reach the shed and Magic steps up to the door and points to a knot hole. "Look."

"What am I looking at?"

"Just put your eye up to the knot hole and look through, almost like you're looking through a kaleidoscope."

I do as he says. "Holy shit," I say under my breath. Cedric is standing in a corner while Marlene paces back and forth. I can see their lips moving but hear nothing. "What is this place?"

"Snow had it built two years ago. It serves as sort of my office. I was being ordered to take care of more and more people, and this makes it easy. It's on our property, which means there's no longer outside forces that can hinder what I have to do. If someone would happen to trespass, all they see is a run-down shed. If the cops ever do come knocking, they won't find anything because all evidence is burnt and then dropped beneath the ground. It's the perfect kill spot."

The moon glints off his eyes as he talks. He loves this shed, or torture space, or office, or whatever the hell he wants to call it. Loves it like he needs it to survive. He's comfortable here, safe. He can do whatever he wants to without consequence. He's not kidding when he says it's the perfect kill spot.

"Does anyone walk away from here?" I ask, already knowing the answer. It isn't Magic's job to spare people, after all.

"No," he confirms. "And tonight is no different, Laney."

I hear the warning in his voice. He's no longer giving me an out, but he's trying to prepare me as much as he can.

"I know."

"Good."

Magic opens the door and that's when I'm able to really see the inside of the shed. It's steel, sterile, and empty other than our captives.

"It's about time you got here," Marlene hisses, cutting off her tirade against Cedric. "I need a bathroom."

I throw back my head and laugh. Magic eyes me skeptically but lets me handle this. When I sober, I look at Cedric.

"You didn't bring a bottle for her?" I tsk, like I'm ashamed of him. "Not a very brotherly thing to do."

"Fuck off you stupid cunt," Cedric sneers.

Magic lunges forward, the machete raised above his head, as if he's going to swing. But he doesn't. "Talk to her like that again, and I won't be able to restrain myself." He looks back at Marlene. "As for you, piss on the floor for all I care."

I step closer to Marlene. She's been relieved of her gun, which takes away all of my fear. She's nothing but a bug I need to squash at this point.

"You should listen to him," I say. "He is holding that really big knife."

Marlene spits in my face. I wipe it away before grabbing her by the shoulders and pulling her upper body down to meet my knee. She cries out in pain and brings her hands to her nose.

Thank you, Snow, for that lesson.

"Don't overdo it, Laney," Magic says. He winks at me to soften the instruction. "You've got the baby to think about."

I smile at him, knowing that he can't help himself. He worries about me. As long as he's not demanding, I'm okay with it. Now if he'd told me to stop and get out because he has to protect me, it'd be an entirely different outcome.

I lift the torch I'm still holding and my heart races. Not

with fear or panic. Nothing like that. It's from excitement and that's the kind of racing heart I can manage.

"Hey, Magic," I call to him. "Remind me again how to use this thing."

I don't need a reminder. I'm well aware of how to use a torch. But our banter back and forth incites panic from our enemies. And quite frankly, it's fun to mentally torture them.

"Twist the knob, hold it to her body, burn." He pauses and then snaps his fingers. "I almost forgot... repeat."

I grab Marlene's hand and hold it tight so she can't get free. Then I go through the motions. When her flesh bubbles and she's screaming, I stop.

"Like that?"

Magic rolls his eyes like I did something wrong. "No, not quite." He glances at Cedric. "Move, I dare you." Then he comes to where I'm standing with Marlene and grabs the torch from me. "Like this."

He holds the torch to her arm, and it doesn't take more than a minute for Marlene's body to go limp as she passes out.

"You're fucking crazy," Cedric accuses. "Jesus, just kill us both and get this over with."

"It's funny, hearing you say that." Magic hands me the torch and returns to Cedric. "If I remember right, you were begging me not to kill you last time."

"And you didn't," Cedric taunts, daring Magic to argue with him.

"And you talk too much."

Magic brings the machete to Cedric's mouth and carves an 'X' over it. Cedric tries to yell, but it's all jumbled with his lips splayed open.

"That's better," Magic quips. He turns back to me. "Now what?"

"Gimme that thing." I reach out for the machete. "I've got an idea."

He hands the weapon to me. I position myself so I'm standing over Marlene. She's still passed out, but I don't care. I just want her dead.

"This is for being a manipulative bitch." I bring the blade down and cut off her right arm. Blood splatter, all over the floor, me, any surface it can reach. "And this is for hurting my brother." I sever her left arm, enjoying the way it feels to inflict so much damage. I move so both my feet are positioned on either side of her body. "And this is because you fucked with the wrong mama bear."

With both hands gripping the handle, I thrust the machete through her chest, bone and all. I stab her over and over again, ignoring the blood now covering me. I keep going, turning her torso into a mass of eviscerated organs. Thrust after thrust, I carve her up. Stab, stab, stab. It feels like an out of body experience, like I'm sitting on a couch, watching a horror flick. All that's missing is the popcorn.

"Laney!" Magic grabs my wrist to stop me. He pries the machete from my hands and pulls me into his chest. "She's dead."

"Not dead enough," I say, winded from my assault. I shove away from Magic and start toward Cedric. "It's your turn."

He tries to take a step back and his eyes widen when he realizes he has nowhere to go. I don't know why he's surprised. He hasn't moved an inch, seemingly paralyzed by the terror of what he just witnessed.

"Magic, can I have the torch, please?" I ask, never taking my eyes off Cedric.

"Laney, maybe I should handle this one."

I hold my hand out, palm up. "Torch. Please."

He sets it in my hand, but when I wrap my fingers around it and flip my hand over, it slips from my grasp. I look down and see my hands coated in blood.

This whole torture business should come with a warning: Slippery when wet.

I wipe the blood on my jeans and then pick the torch up off the floor. This time, I'm able to keep a hold on it.

"I'm going to ask you a few questions, Cedric." I take a step closer. "I don't expect you to talk, but I do expect you to be honest." I twist the knob on the torch and the flame comes to life. "Understand?"

He nods.

"Good. First question: Were you and the dearly departed really going to kidnap my son today?" He frantically shakes his head. "And here I thought you understood."

I hold the torch to his knee until he starts nodding.

"See, that wasn't so hard, was it? Next question: Are you doing this because you actually give a shit about Shiloh?"

At first, it seems as if he's not going to answer, but then he shakes his head.

"Wow, that's a first for you. Being honest without a little incentive."

Magic steps up beside me and I watch him out of the corner of my eye. He surveys Cedric, as if inspecting my work.

"I've got a few questions of my own," he says. "Care if I take a turn?"

I try to hand the torch to Magic, but he doesn't take it.

"I won't be needing that."

He launches an assault on Cedric, landing blow after blow like he's at the gym and Cedric is the punching bag.

200

Cedric collapses in a heap on the floor but Magic doesn't let up. He straddles him and continues to deliver right-handed jabs until Cedric manages to get his arms up to block them.

His face is barely recognizable with the amount of swelling, blood, and bruising.

"That..." Magic spits on him. "... is for living." He stands and turns to face me. "I'm done."

"Great." I spread Cedric's legs with my foot and squat between them. If his eyes weren't swollen shut, I imagine they'd be wide as saucers. I pat his leg with my free hand. "Don't worry, it's almost over. I only have one more question."

Cedric manages to nod.

"Are you sorry?" He doesn't answer, and I shift the torch closer to the knee I burnt earlier. "Answer me, Cedric. And remember, you lie, I burn."

He hesitates for another few seconds and then nods. I don't believe him, of course, because the only thing Cedric Milner is sorry for is getting caught. I back the torch away, giving him a brief moment full of a false hope.

"Right, and maybe I'll be the next First Lady."

I shove the torch against his balls and Cedric howls. The smell of searing flesh fills my nostrils and bile crawls up the back of my throat. I swallow it down, refusing to stop.

"Say hello to the Devil for me."

I shift the torch slightly and push it forward. Finally, *finally*, Cedric passes out. He held out longer than I would have guessed, I'll give him that.

I twist the knob again and toss the torch onto the floor. Magic helps me stand and twists me around to face him.

"You know he's not dead yet, right?"

"I know. You can kill him. Get your revenge for him surviving before."

Magic settles his lips against mine. The kiss deepens, a metallic taste mingling with saliva. But I don't dare pull away. It's settling my racing heart, making me feel whole for the first time in months.

Eventually, all good things must come to an end. Fortunately, it's not the end of us.

"What now?" I ask.

Magic drags me to the door, and we step out into the dark night. The air feels good on my sticky skin and cools my burning flesh. He drops my hand and goes to the corner of the shed, where he pulls a lever.

Back at my side, he directs me to the knot hole. Now that I know what it really is, I look through it, and grin.

"Now, Laney, we watch 'em burn."

EPILOGUE

MAGIC

Two and a half months later...

"You're doing great."

I wipe the sweat from Laney's forehead. She's been in active labor for nine hours and it's starting to take a toll on her. She's exhausted, sweaty, and in pain. If I could do this for her, I would, but I'd have opted for the drugs.

"I can't," Laney pants, dropping back onto the hospital bed. "I'm done, Doc. Just pull her out."

Dr. Dryer chuckles. "No can do." She reaches up and presses on Laney's stomach. "You beat cancer so I know you can do this."

Laney shakes her head violently. "Nope. I want drugs. Give me the drugs," she begs.

"You're almost there," Dr. Dryer assures her. "Okay, here we go, I need you to push."

"C'mon, Laney, you've got this."

Laney squeezes my hand as another contraction takes over. She's got quite a grip on her. I've remained her cheerleader through the entire process, but even I can only be so strong.

"That's it, bear down," Dr. Dryer prods. When the contraction stops, she lifts her head to look at Laney. "One more, mama. When I say so, push, okay?"

Laney looks at me. "Magic, I can't. I'm sorry, but it's too much. I can't—"

"Push, push, push."

Laney immediately reacts and bears down. The groans and grunts that come from her mouth can only be described as something other than human. Despite all that, she's still the sexiest woman I've ever met. And bringing new life into the world only makes her more magnificent.

A loud cry fills the room.

"Congrats Mom and Dad." Dr. Dryer lifts our daughter up so we can see her. "Ten fingers and ten toes. Absolutely perfect." She hands the baby off to a nurse. "We'll get her cleaned up and then you can hold her."

Laney's eyes light up, the last nine hours apparently forgotten. And I guess, in a way, they are. All that matters now is that our little girl is healthy, and she's here, in the flesh.

A nurse lays our daughter on Laney's chest. With my arms around Laney, and her arms around the baby, the rest of the world disappears.

"Hi Zoe," Laney says softly. "I'm your mommy." She points to me. "And that's your daddy."

"Zoe, my baby girl." My eyes become misty, and I swipe at the tear that spills onto my cheek. "It's wonderful to finally meet you."

"Doc was right, she is perfect."

I press a kiss to Laney's forehead. "Just like you."

Laney's eyes droop, the exhaustion taking over. I lift Zoe from her arms and cradle the newborn to my chest.

"Get some sleep, Mama. We'll be here when you wake up."

Laney doesn't fight it and within minutes, her breathing is deep and even. The nurse comes back in to check on her. She takes her vitals, checks the IV, and smiles.

"Everything looks good." Then her eyes travel from my face to my chest, where Zoe rests. But she doesn't stop there, like I expect. She lowers them to my waist and that's where she stops. "Real good."

When she brings her head back up, her face is flushed. I nod toward Laney and then lift Zoe slightly. "Never gonna happen."

The nurse chuckles nervously. "Right. Sorry." She checks Laney's vitals again, although it seems more out of nervous energy than anything else. "There are a lot of people in the waiting room. I assume, based on your matching vests that they're with you?"

"Are they getting a little rowdy, like caged bulls dying to break free?"

"A little."

"Then yes, they're with me." I peer down at Zoe, who's starting to fuss. "Can you let them in? I promise, when they're done meeting Zoe, they'll scatter and get out of your hair."

"Sure. But they can't stay long."

"That's fine. Thanks."

The nurse leaves, but it isn't long before I hear my rowdy brothers. Their footsteps are loud and fast.

Oh hell, please tell me they aren't running.

"There she is."

I face Snow and press a finger to my lips.

"Sorry," he whispers as he reaches out his arms for Zoe. "Here, hand her over."

Snow holds Zoe as if she's a bomb that might explode if he's not careful. It'd be comical if I didn't feel exactly like that when I hold her.

"So, brother, what's her name?" Duck asks, stepping up to peek at my daughter.

Heather is beside him, and her eyes fill with tears. "She's beautiful."

"Thanks. And Zoe. Her name is Zoe. It's Greek for 'fighter'."

Everyone takes turns holding Zoe. I watch as these big, burly, ready for battle men turn into puddles of mush when she's in their arms. The power this little girl holds is immense. And she's less than an hour old.

"Oh," Dip begins. "I finally heard back from our inside guy at the police station. Nothing on Cedric, Marlene, or any of their aliases. We're in the clear."

"What if someone does end up filing a missing person's report?" I ask, needing to know. They don't know the extent of Laney's involvement in their deaths, but I do. And I will do whatever it takes to keep her name off the cop's radar.

"Already took care of that. Paid him to make sure that if anything turns up, it gets buried. You're good, Magic. Nothing to worry about."

I hope you're right.

"Hi guys."

We all turn to look at Laney. She scoots up in the bed and holds her arms out. "Give me my daughter." Laney's smiling, but her tone has a hint of a threat in it.

Toga hands Zoe to her mother and backs up. "Congrats, Laney."

"Thanks," she says, not bothering to look at anyone but Zoe.

Snow goes to the side of the bed and rests a hand on Laney's shoulder. "Great job, Laney. I'm proud of you."

"I'm pretty proud of myself too." She raises her head, concern filling her stare. "Shiloh. How's he doing?"

Snow chuckles. "He's fine. Chompin' at the bit to get here and meet his baby sister. Sami and I will bring him back in the morning. It's late, and I'm hoping he and Lennox are both in bed by the time I get home."

"Tell him I..." She glances at me. "Tell him *we* love him."

"I will." He leans over and kisses her on the cheek. "Get some rest. I love you."

"Love you too." She looks at the others. "All of you."

A round of 'I love you too's are spoken, and each brother takes their turn kissing Laney and Zoe goodbye. If I weren't as trusting as I am of them, I'd be kicking them all in their teeth. But I know I have nothing to worry about. They love her as much as I do, in a brotherly way, and who am I to deny her that?

The room clears out until all that remains is our little family... well, most of it. The picture will be complete when Shiloh gets here tomorrow.

"So, when are we getting married?" I ask Laney.

I proposed a few weeks after our time in the shed, but she told me to ask again after Zoe was born. I don't know if this is what she had in mind when she said it, but I refuse to wait any longer.

"It's killing you, isn't it?"

"What? Is it so bad that I want to marry you?"

"I wasn't talking about that." She smiles. "It's killing you that Duck beat you to the punch? That he and Heather are engaged before we are?"

"Fine, maybe a little bit. But that's not why I'm asking you now."

"I know."

"So..."

"Of course I'll marry you." Her smile widens. "As long as Shiloh says 'yes' when you ask him tomorrow."

"He will," I say, my tone cocky. "He loves me."

"Yeah, he does. And so do I."

Zoe starts crying but Laney is able to quickly calm her down. When Zoe's eyes drift closed, Laney turns to look out the window.

"What's wrong?" I ask, recognizing the far away stare she gets when she's worried about something.

She swivels her head, without lifting it from the pillow, to look at me. "What if we're not ready for this? I mean, calming her down, protecting her? It's easy now. But what about later, as she grows and is more immersed in the world? Can we protect her from the world, Magic?"

I brush Laney's hair behind her ear and cup her cheek. "I think the better question is whether or not the world is ready for her."

I rest my free hand on Zoe's head.

"Because if she's anything like her mom, the world better watch out."

Next in the Satan's Legacy MC Series

Duck's Salvation

Duck...

I finally have the life I want: an amazing fiancée, a baby on the way, Satan's Legacy MC as my family. And then an accident, or my own stupidity, changes the course of my life forever. Unable to look at me, my fiancé removes herself from the picture, leaving me with a premature baby who requires more love and care than I know how to give.

As I struggle to cope with it all, the last thing I need is some chick trying to do and say what she thinks are all the right things. No, I want to wallow in self-pity and go on a violent spree that will take the edge off the pain. The problem is, no matter how much I try to dull my emotions and fortify my walls against her, she doesn't back down. And just when I realize I'm fighting a losing battle and need her in my life, trouble shows up at my door, threatening to shatter the new life I'm creating.

Grace...

Nursing was something I grew up knowing I wanted to do. And then my own tragedy struck, and it made my job less fulfilling. Until one night, when a biker and his fiancée show up at the ER, and I watch as their lives fall apart, much like mine did a few years ago.

When I realize the fiancée is gone, but he's still there, I can't help but want to ease his pain. It emanates from him in waves, and every single reason I wanted to be a nurse kicks back in, forcing me to do whatever it takes to help him through the worst days of his life. But it's clear he wants nothing to do with me. No matter... I will break through his defenses, one way or another. Not even his vengeful past, intent on haunting him, will stop me.

About the Author

Andi Rhodes is an author whose passion is creating romance from chaos in all her books! She writes MC (motorcycle club) romance with a generous helping of suspense and doesn't shy away from the more difficult topics. Her books can be triggering for some so consider yourself warned. Andi also ensures each book ends with the couple getting their HEA! Most importantly, Andi is living her real life HEA with her husband and their boxers.

For access to release info, updates, and exclusive content, be sure to sign up for Andi's newsletter at andirhodes.com.

Also by Andi Rhodes

Broken Rebel Brotherhood

Broken Souls

Broken Innocence

Broken Boundaries

Broken Rebel Brotherhood: Complete Series Box set

Broken Rebel Brotherhood: Next Generation

Broken Hearts

Broken Wings

Broken Mind

Bastards and Badges

Stark Revenge

Slade's Fall

Jett's Guard

Soulless Kings MC

Fender

Joker

Piston

Greaser

Riker

Trainwreck

Squirrel

Gibson

Satan's Legacy MC

Snow's Angel

Toga's Demons

Magic's Torment